LIQUID DEATH

The hunters formed like a pack of dogs and came running. Jessie fired both rounds of her derringer into the moving mass. One of the killers grunted with pain and skidded in the dirt. The others scattered and began to return fire. Jessie ducked back around the corner as bullets ate into the brick building.

She removed the cotton wadding from around the vial of nitroglycerine. Her hand shook a little as she raised and cocked it, thinking that she would have to make a smooth throwing motion or the explosive might go off in her own hand.

She took a deep breath.

Jessie leaned back out into the alley and hurled the vial with a long throw using all of her strength. Jessie threw herself backward and covered her ears as the explosion ripped through the alley. . . .

Also in the LONE STAR series from Jove

◂•WESLEY ELLIS•▸

LONE STAR

AND THE SIERRA SABOTAGE

JOVE BOOKS, NEW YORK

LONE STAR AND THE SIERRA SABOTAGE

A Jove Book/published by arrangement with
the author

PRINTING HISTORY
Jove edition/January 1991

ISBN: 0-515-10495-7

Jove Books are published by The Berkley Publishing Group,
200 Madison Avenue, New York, New York 10016. The name
"JOVE"and the "J" logo are trademarks belonging
to Jove Publications, Inc.

PRINTED IN THE UNITED STATES OF AMERICA

10 9 8 7 6 5 4 3 2 1

LONE STAR

AND THE SIERRA SABOTAGE

Chapter 1

Jessica Starbuck and her samurai, Ki, stood beside their saddle horses and watched the Irish as they slammed down the heavy steel rails for the Union Pacific Railroad. The workers had settled down into a rhythm of tracklaying that was beautiful to behold and that carried them westward at a rate of more than five miles a day.

To Jessie, the laying of track had become a ballet of muscle and steel. First, sixteen rails were loaded off a heavy railroad supply car and placed on a light track-cart pulled by a single horse, which galloped forward. The cart was met by men who yanked the rails off in pairs and, on command, slammed them down on the new ties exactly four feet, eight-and-one-half inches apart. No sooner did the rails crunch down upon the new roadbed than muscular spike men would swing their hammers and nail the rails down tight. Couplers would attach what were called "fish plates" to bind the rails end to end, preventing them from shifting laterally, before jumping aside as another pair of rails was hauled forward and dropped exactly into place.

"It's a thing of beauty to watch," Jessie said, with an

1

admiring shake of her pretty head.

The superintendant of construction nodded, "Thanks to you and the samurai thwarting those saboteurs, we can concentrate on racing across Wyoming and Utah Territory and not worrying about being blown up at every trestle and tunnel. We are in a race with the Central Pacific, and we mean to drive all the way across Nevada and join them in Reno."

"That's a tall order," Jessie said. "Where are they right now?"

"Still stuck on the western slopes of the Sierra Nevadas," Butler said. "Did you hear that their Irish went on strike, and so Crocker and his superintendent, Strobridge, went to San Francisco and hired Chinamen!"

Ki was half-American and half-Japanese, but he did not appreciate the tone of derision he now heard. "The Chinese are a very industrious people," he said. "They also are brave, don't fight like your Irish, and won't drink anything stronger than tea. I'll bet you wish your men were as clean living."

The superintendent frowned. "Listen, Ki, I meant no insult to those Celestials, it's just that they're too damn small to lift rails, swing a pick and work a shovel."

"They were strong enough to build the Great Wall of China."

Butler's face flushed with embarrassment. "Okay," he said, "I stand corrected. But point of the matter is that I'll match my Irish against those Chinamen any old day. You won't see them laying track like my men. No sir! They won't compare to the miles that this crew will rack up day after day."

Ki decided that arguing with this man was a waste of time and breath.

Jessie tightened the cinch on her horse. "I guess we

2

had better ride. I've got some ranch land up on the Powder River to—"

Before Jessie could finish, the Union Pacific's telegraph operator came rushing up waving a telegram for his boss. "Mr. Benton!"

"What is it?" the superintendant asked sternly, for he was not a man who appreciated interruptions.

"Thought you had better see this right away," the operator said, puffing with exertion.

Benton took the telegram and his brow furrowed with concern. He handed the message to Jessie, saying, "Looks like the masterminds who were trying to destroy this railroad have shifted to the Central Pacific."

Jessie read the telegram out loud for Ki's benefit.

"FIRST CENTRAL PACIFIC TUNNEL AT DONNER PASS COLLAPSES. SIXTEEN CHINESE BURIED ALIVE. SABOTAGE SUSPECTED."

"This shouldn't surprise any of us," the samurai said quietly. "Whoever failed here in Wyoming only has to succeed in the Sierra Nevadas and they will have defeated the transcontinental railroad dream."

"That's right," Butler said grimly. "My God, though! Hasn't there been enough killing! What demented minds are behind all this?"

"That's a question we may never be able to answer," Jessie said. "We were lucky enough to beat them at this end, but we never even came close to uncovering the ringleaders."

"You said it was foreigners," Butler reminded her.

"I only said that I found *evidence* of them," Jessie corrected. "And I suspect that it is the same kind of powerful international cartel that attempted to recruit my father years ago into their evil plan to collapse

3

the American banking system and create international chaos in the financial markets. Failing to recruit him, they killed him."

"But what would anyone have to gain by sabotaging our first transcontinental?" Butler asked. "What could they be after?"

"Money and power," Jessie said. "For example, what if they simply want to make things so difficult that Congress will throw up its hands in exasperation and cancel the transcontinental project? That would mean millions of dollars would be gained or lost, depending on if you were a freight or stageline or even one of the hundreds of towns and banks that stand to win or lose depending on the final outcome of this bold adventure."

"Yeah," Butler said quietly. "I can see that. But that still doesn't begin to explain a possible foreign involvement in America's affairs. That's the part I don't understand."

"Foreign interests might have speculated heavily in cheap land, intending that Congress would reroute this line and they'd reap fortunes. Or there may be powerful interests at work in Dixie. You know, there are many Southerners who will never accept that the Confederacy was defeated. Greedy foreign powers would not hesitate to exploit Southern hate and bitterness for their own gain."

"It's all too complex for me," Butler admitted. "I'm just an engineer trying to lay track across some of the roughest country God ever created."

Jessie mounted her horse and studied the samurai. She looked at home in the saddle and her long, shapely legs gripped the barrel of her horse with confidence, but her expression was pensive.

"What's wrong?" Ki asked, reading the worry in her pretty green eyes.

"How can we *not* go to California and attempt to help Mr. Crocker defeat whoever is behind all this terror?" Jessie asked.

Ki understood what was coming next. "When we left your Circle Star Ranch, you told your foreman we'd be back in a month or two at the most. It's been longer than that already."

"I know, I know," Jessie said. "We left in the spring, and I missed the complete roundup for the third year in a row. But Ed Wright is a capable man, and he probably does better without my interference."

"Maybe," Ki said. "But if we go to California, we've got some hard riding in the weeks to come. And don't forget about the Paiute Indians. They shut down the Pony Express back in 1860. The Paiute haven't gotten any friendlier."

"You could swing way south around them," Butler offered.

But Jessie shook her head. "No. That would take us into the heart of the Nevada and Utah deserts and many miles out of our way. We'll head straight for Reno."

"I knew that was coming," the samurai said.

"And you welcome the challenge," Jessie said. "You are always happiest when we are riding into trouble and unsure of what we'll be facing."

Ki did not even try to deny the fact. He was samurai, and his worst times were those when he was idle down at Circle Star, Jessie's immense Texas cattle ranch.

"What kind of a person is this Crocker's number one man?" Jessie asked, because Strobridge was the man whose cooperation they would most need.

"Never met Harvey Strobridge," Butler said. "Hope

5

I never do. From what I heard, he's a tall, ugly New Englander who drives his men like dogs and cusses worse than a drunken sailor. He's an impatient bastard, too. Got in so much of a hurry out of Sacramento that he couldn't wait for a keg of black powder to explode."

"What happened to him?" Jessie asked.

"Lost one of his eyes!" Butler shook his head. "I understand the Chinese call him the 'One Eye Bossy Man,' and the few Irish that didn't quit and leave call him names that I wouldn't repeat to a lady."

Jessie glanced at Ki. They were not pleased to hear this kind of talk. But Harvey Strobridge was Butler's counterpart on the rival railroad, and Jessie hoped that this fact unfairly colored Butler's description and opinion of the Central Pacific construction boss.

Butler wasn't finished. "I've also heard that Charles Crocker himself is as vile-tongued as Strobridge. 'Course, he might be in Washington, D.C., a lot, trying to fight for government funds the same as our own Union Pacific executives. Government money is the lifeblood of this challenge, and Congress is as tightfisted as ever."

"Of course," Jessie said. She looked to the west and thought about all the hard miles they'd have to go. Texas sounded good, but she knew that she'd never forgive herself if she didn't even try to get to the bottom of whatever or whoever was behind this attempt to destroy America's best hope for a railroad linking the West to the East.

"Wish us luck," Jessie said.

"You'll need more than luck just to get across the Nevada Territory with your scalp," Butler predicted gravely. "But in case you do, I could telegraph Crocker and tell him you're coming."

"Better not," Jessie decided. "This time, I think we'll just go in and see what happens."

She waved good-bye and then touched spurs to her horse, wishing it were her own palomino, Sun, instead of a Union Pacific mount. In fairness, however, Butler had given both her and Ki his best horses, and now the success or failure to reach California's Donner Pass was up to Jessie and her samurai.

Jessie felt the wind brush at her face as she and Ki galloped stirrup to stirrup. When she glanced sideways, the samurai was actually smiling with anticipation of the adventures and, yes, even the obstacles that they would soon encounter. But Ki was samurai and *ninja*. He lived to fight and protect her and considered it his karma.

But isn't it also mine? Jessie asked herself, aware that her own heart was beating fast.

Of course it was! Her Circle Star Ranch could run itself under the expert guidance of her foreman. But the transcontinental railroad might be destroyed if she and Ki did not finally root out the evil that stood in the path of its completion.

Yes, Jessie thought, this is my karma as well. In less than two days they would be galloping across the immense Bridger Basin, and then they'd race over the Continental Divide at South Pass and head for Utah Territory and the Great Salt Lake Basin.

Jessie had never been to the heart of the Mormon stronghold, and she supposed that meeting Brigham Young would just have to wait for another day. They'd be in one big hurry to get through Paiute country and attack the Sierra Nevada Mountains just west of Reno.

And somewhere on the other side of those huge mountains, near a place called Donner Pass, which had been

7

the site of one of the West's most horrifying tragedies, Chinese were being murdered and buried alive because of a terrible and sinister plot. It was a challenge plenty worthy of a samurai and a tall Texas cowgirl.

Chapter 2

Jessie and Ki pushed their horses hard for the first two hundred miles, and when they camped beside the Green River in western Wyoming, they noticed that the colors of fall were already starting to turn the aspen and cottonwood trees into brilliant autumn foliage.

She could also see snow capping the highest peaks of the northern Wind River Mountains, and it occurred to her that the Central Pacific Railroad would soon be facing the bitter winter that made crossing Donner Pass all but impossible. How on earth, she wondered, did Strobridge, Crocker and the others think that they could defeat those towering mountains and incredible summit snows?

Ki had been watching her. "You're worrying about the Sierras already, aren't you?"

"Yes. I can't imagine how a railroad could build over them and, even if they do, how they could keep any kind of train schedule during the winter months. Why, I've heard that the snow at Donner Pass can get sixty feet or more deep, and blizzards are not uncommon."

Ki thought about that for several minutes. "My guess is that the Central Pacific will be forced to tunnel under the summit. I'm sure that's where our saboteurs figure to strike."

"Yes," Jessie agreed. "And apparently, they've already been successful."

After two very, very long days in the saddle, they decided to rest their horses and get to sleep early. Tomorrow night, they'd be climbing the eastern slopes of the high Wasatch Mountains and their animals would need all their strength.

Jessie and Ki lay under the stars that night, each locked in a comfortable, weary silence. Jessie thought about how she and Ki had been through so many difficult scrapes and always somehow managed to emerge victorious. It was mostly, she knew, due to the samurai's courage and resourcefulness. But mine, too, she thought, remembering how her father had trained her as a child to be resourceful and an expert marksman. She could handle the gun strapped on her hip about as well as any but the professional gunfighters, and when it came to making a rifle bark with authority, Jessie felt very confident.

Stars blanketed the heavens, but the moon was barely a sliver and the night was inky black. A cool breeze swept down from the mountains, and their horses were hobbled and grazing in the meadow.

Their campfire was burning low, and Jessie was just about to drift off to sleep when she heard one of the horses whinny in fear. Instantly, she and the samurai were jumping to their feet, grabbing their weapons.

Ki had his bow and arrows, Jessie her Winchester, and they were staring into the darkness when they heard a terrible roar and one of the horses whinnied again in terror. The sound of hoofbeats was followed closely by the awful sound of a dying animal being dragged to the earth.

"He's got our horses!" Jessie cried, starting out into the night.

"No!" the samurai yelled, grabbing her and pulling her back toward their dying fire. "Out there he'd have all the advantage."

"But our horses!"

"Listen," Ki ordered. "One is still trying to get away."

They could hear it thumping across the meadow. Horses or mules became very adept at hopping rapidly out of danger, even while wearing hobbles.

Another roar behind them caused Jessie and Ki to spin around. Ki already had an arrow nocked on his bowstring and Jessie a bullet levered and ready to fire.

But the night fell dead silent and they could hear nothing.

"I'll put some more wood on the fire," Jessie said, setting her rifle down and then turning to grab a thick branch.

Jessie's hand had not yet closed around the branch when a grizzly as big as a longhorn steer attacked the camp with an awesome burst of speed. The samurai drew back his bowstring and fired in one fluid motion even before the grizzly was clearly visible. His powerful bow spun 180 degrees, but before it had completed that arc, Ki was already nocking and unleashing a second arrow.

Ki's mind did not register the fact that the immense carnivorous grizzly was bearing down on him with every intention of ripping his head from his shoulders. There was no room for panic, and the samurai's movements were automatic, because he had mastered the art of *ignashi*, the style of rapid firing in which a samurai bowman could unleash his arrows faster than a man could lever and fire a well-oiled Winchester.

The attacking grizzly, however, was demented in its

11

purpose, and its heavy layer of summer fat protected its body, so that the samurai's arrows did not penetrate as deeply as they should have, and the grizzly was able to reach Ki and crush him between its massive forearms.

Ki's hand groped for his knife even as the bear's jaws locked on his shoulder and ripped flesh away to the bone. Ki struggled to retain consciousness. He grabbed his long, thin, *tanto* blade and probed deeply for the heart of the savage creature that was about to kill him.

The plunging knife cut through vitals and the great beast actually screamed in Ki's face, filling the samurai's nostrils with its hot, fetid breath. Again and again Ki stabbed deeply until his mind threatened to lose consciousness, and the creature released its bite, and its great forearms relented in their rib-crushing pressure.

But even then, the grizzly might have torn Ki's throat out except that Jessie picked herself up, shoved her rifle's muzzle against the grizzly's side and pulled the trigger.

The bear howled in death, and its bloody fangs gnashed at the slice of moon before it collapsed into the fire, body violated by arrows, a rifle bullet and the *tanto* blade.

Ki staggered back with blood pouring from his left shoulder. He felt dizzy and suddenly very weak.

Jessie caught him. "You're going to be all right," she said over and over.

"I know that."

"But I've got to get this shoulder to stop bleeding. Can you still wiggle your fingers?"

Ki moved his fingers, knowing that Jessie was concerned about nerve damage. He was strong enough to push himself away from the fire. The grizzly's fur had caught ablaze; it was smoking and smelled terrible.

Jessie pulled off her coat and then her blouse, which she tore into strips. "If I don't wash this out well before

12

I get the bleeding stopped, it will probably cause infection."

"If you don't stop the bleeding now," Ki said gently, "infection won't be a problem, because I'll have bled to death."

Jessie agreed and began to wind the strips she had torn around Ki's shoulder. "They've got to be very tight," she said.

Ki was struggling to retain consciousness. His vision was blurring, and the stars overhead seemed to be making a lazy spinning motion. There was something Ki knew he needed to tell Jessie in case he lost consciousness, but it seemed to take him forever to remember what it was.

Finally, he remembered. "There's another bear out there," Ki mumbled. "It might come looking for its friend."

"I don't think so," Jessie said. "Not when it smells its friend's hair burning."

The samurai actually smiled. "I guess you're probably right about that. But this is a bad break, Jessie. I'm not going to be as much help for. . . ."

"That's not important!" Jessie lowered her voice, embarrassed to have let her anxiety get the better of her. She forced a smile and touched Ki's cheek. "Listen, if you hadn't knocked me aside and jumped forward, *I'd* have been the one that the grizzly landed on, instead of you. Now, I've got to get this bleeding stopped, and then we'll worry about how to get help come morning."

Ki nodded. He closed his eyes and whispered, "Just in case, though, reload your rifle and keep it close. There's no accounting for what grizzly will do when they smell fresh blood."

Jessie knew the advice was sound, but she wasn't about to divert her attention to the rifle until she had the samurai's shoulder bound up tightly enough to stop the bleeding.

Several minutes later, she guessed she'd succeeded. The samurai had lapsed into unconsciousness, and his face and upper body were covered with blood.

Jessie found her canteen and wiped her own hands and forearms clean, then carefully bathed Ki's upper body. The job took her almost an hour, and by then she could see that the samurai was pretty well ripped up in several places. His left arm, for instance, had been clawed and had deep furrows in it from the elbow to the back of his hand. There were more claw marks on his chest, and Jessie wondered if any of his ribs had been crushed by the grizzly.

Finally satisfied that she had done everything possible for Ki, Jessie covered him with her own blanket, then pulled her coat on and turned to see the burning bear.

What am I going to do tomorrow? she asked herself. The nearest help is probably more than a hundred miles away, in Salt Lake City, unless I'm lucky enough to stumble on some mountain man or hermit out prospecting in these mountains.

Jessie expelled a deep sigh and looked up at the stars again, as if they might give her some answers or, failing that, at least comfort her with their cold beauty.

She knew that in the morning she would have to leave the samurai and go searching for their second horse in the hope that it had not been overtaken and slaughtered. Jessie prayed that it had gotten away. Without at least one horse to pull a travois, she knew things were desperate indeed.

Chapter 3

Jessie awoke chilled and unrefreshed. She supposed she had slept sometime during the night, but it could not have been for more than a few fitful hours. Now, a cold, predawn light was poking over the eastern hills and her campfire was barely smoking.

She stood up and reached for the canteen. Pouring a little water into her cupped hand, she washed the sleep from her eyes and then staggered over to study the samurai. He looked uncharacteristically pale, but when Jessie reached out and measured his pulse, it was strong and steady.

"I'll live to ride the Central Pacific over the Sierra Nevada Mountains," Ki said, opening his eyes and looking up into her face.

Jessie smiled. "Of course you will. But I'm worried about getting us out of here and finding a doctor. You've heard how these kinds of wounds can become infected. You need some medical help."

"You did pretty well all by yourself last night," Ki said in a weak voice.

"Thanks, but I don't have any medicine and that's what we need right now."

"No," Ki corrected, "what we really need is that runaway horse. You're going to have to go hunt him up. If he isn't bear bait by now, he's the key."

Jessie knew that the samurai was right, but the idea of leaving Ki alone and in such poor shape was not at all to her liking. For one thing, the grizzly might return.

"Go on," Ki said. "Have something to eat and then take the rifle and go find that horse."

"I'll go," Jessie said, "but only if you agree that you'll keep the rifle. You sure can't use your bow and arrows with that shoulder of yours."

Ki started to protest, but Jessie placed her fingers over his lips and said, "Remember who's the boss and who works for whom. You're keeping my rifle or I'm staying here. Besides, I have a six-gun, and you know that I'm plenty capable of using it."

Ki knew that he had lost the argument. Jessie wasn't bluffing. Unless he agreed to her terms, she was stubborn enough to stick to her words and remain right by his side. That wouldn't do either of them any good. They were not exactly on a well-traveled road, and it could be weeks before anyone came along who could help them. Ki simply did not want things to progress that far downhill. In weeks, he might be dead, if the bear's fangs and claws had poisoned his flesh.

"All right," he said. "I'll take the rifle, but you have to promise to keep going west until you either find the horse or reach help. There's no point in both of us staying here waiting for the worst to happen."

Jessie stood up and shoved her hands deep into her pockets. "Agreed," she said finally.

An hour later, she had done everything possible to make the samurai comfortable. Still, Jessie lingered, hesitating to go.

16

Ki took a drink from the canteen she had refilled and left at his side. "If you're lucky, that damned Union Pacific saddle horse will be alive and grazing over the next hill, but if he isn't, just walk as strong as you can for as long as you can."

"I will," she promised. They were following a trail that lead them straight for the Wasatch Mountains. "How far do you figure Salt Lake City to be?"

"Not over a hundred miles," he said. "But my guess is that you'll come upon someone long before that."

"I'm sure you're right," Jessie said, lifting her chin. "I'll just have to keep moving."

"Jessie?" She looked down quickly at him. "Listen to me," he said in a quiet, serious voice. "Don't push yourself too hard. Don't use up all your reserves so that, if trouble comes, you've nothing left to give."

Jessie nodded her head, then crouched down and touched his forehead. "You've already got a fever. I'm going to find that horse or another and get you to a doctor in a hurry. I promise."

The samurai felt something hard knot up in his throat. "Just don't let another grizzly have the next dance with you," he said. "And watch out for any renegade Indians."

"They're the ones that had better watch out," Jessie said, standing up and then starting off directly toward the eastern mountains.

Ki watched her stride out of their camp, and he felt a strong rush of admiration. Jessie was long-legged and moved like a sleek cat. Her walk, even now when she was hurried and half-sick worrying over him, was sensual.

"She'll make it," he whispered to himself. "Even without me to watch out for her, she'll make it."

Two miles east of camp, Jessie found the second horse where it had finally been pulled down by the grizzly. Her

17

green eyes flashed with anger, and she studied the dead animal for several minutes before she walked around it, and kept moving east.

All that day, she paced herself, walking for two hours, resting for thirty minutes. By nightfall, however, she was staggering with weariness.

The moon again gave her no light, and even the stars seemed stingy with their glow. Jessie found a cluster of boulders and squeezed into a crack where no grizzly could reach her without getting shot between the eyes.

In the morning, she finished off the last of her food, and when she saw a rabbit about noon, she drew and fired in one smooth motion. She wasted little time in making her fire and cooking the rabbit over the coals of pinecones, and it proved to be delicious.

It was nearing the evening the second day of her trek when she passed over a high, windswept ridge and saw a magnificent hidden lake that was nestled in what she was certain was the cradle of a long-extinct volcano. The dying sun had laid a sheen of gold and crimson across the rippling waters, and Jessie, despite her troubled mind and body, was calmed by the sight of such pristine beauty.

Weary to the point of collapse from her hard climb up the eastern slopes of the Wasatch, she found a rock and paused to enjoy the view and to catch her breath.

It was then that she saw another wonderful sight, and that was of a man in a canoe who came paddling around a point of land and then beached his craft and shouldered a heavy pack. Jessie leapt to her feet and jumped up on a high rock to shout, "Hello down there!"

Her voice carried strongly over the crater, and it caused the man to swing around suddenly, drop the huge bundle he was carrying and throw a rifle to his shoulder.

Even though Jessie was waving her arms, the man spotted her high up on the mountainside, took aim and fired!

The blast of his powerful rifle filled the crater, and Jessie heard the man's bullet strike a rock not fifteen feet downslope. It was an incredible feat of marksmanship, and had the distance been only slightly less, Jessie was sure that she would have been drilled squarely.

She threw herself down from the rock and shouted, "Don't shoot, I need your help! I . . . I can pay for help!"

She saw the man lower his rifle and then he bellowed, "You a damn white woman?"

The question caught her by surprise and Jessie was momentarily at a loss for words. "Yes," she finally called. "But what does that have to do with anything?"

He didn't bother to answer her question. He didn't bother to even look up at her again as he grabbed his pack and marched into the forest.

"Wait a minute!" Jessie called. "Please, you've got to help me."

"No, ma'am, I sure as hell don't!" he hollered from the forest.

Jessie swore to herself in anger and helpless rage. Of all of them she might have found, why this one? Why not some intelligent, friendly and Christian fellow who had the decency to help and be helped?

But Jessie knew that she would have no such man and that Ki's very life might depend on her success or failure in recruiting this man's assistance. So she hurried on down the steep mountainside until she came to the lake, and then she followed the man's tracks up into the trees and had no trouble locating his rough, one-room cabin.

19

The bundle he had been carrying turned out to be the hindquarters of an elk, and now the man was preparing a fire to cook meat and smoke jerky.

"Excuse me," Jessie said, "but we need to talk."

"I don't need to talk at all," he said, looking up at her directly for the first time.

Jessie was surprised to see that he was much, much older than she had imagined from the fluid way he moved and the size of the bundle he could tote.

His face was deeply lined, clean-shaven except for a long, droopy mustache that was pure silver to match his bushy eyebrows. He might have been sixty, but he was a well-preserved old codger.

"I don't need help for myself," she said, walking up to stand before him. "I'm not lost and I can take care of my own troubles."

He was hacking away at the chunks of meat. "That a fact?"

"Yes."

"Strange to see a woman dressed in a man's ridin' britches and work shirt. You're wearin' riding boots, too. Not too damn good for walkin', now are they?"

"No," Jessie said, feeling the sting of blisters. "They aren't. But until two days ago, my friend and I were on horseback. We made camp on the Green River and were attacked at night by grizzly."

"They'll do it sometimes," the old mountain man said. "You kin see the same one a hundred times, and he'll ignore you until all of a sudden, he just takes a queer twist of mind and wants to have you for supper."

"Yes," Jessie said. "Well, the grizzly killed our horses and badly injured my friend. I left him on the Green and struck out for Salt Lake City."

"What the hell for?"

20

Jessie was taken aback by the man's sharp question. "Well . . . I didn't know where else to look for a doctor and medicine."

"Griz chew him up pretty good, huh?"

"Yes, I'm afraid so. Maybe broke a few of his ribs, too. I got the bleeding stopped, but I know that the wounds will suppurate and poison his blood without a doctor's attention."

"And you think that the Mormon will help him, him not being one of their persuasion?"

Jessie's voice took on a hard edge. "He's a human being and so are they. They'd help him whether he was of their faith or not."

"Balls!"

Jessie ground her teeth in silence. She knew something about the Mormon people, and while they were clannish, they were also very decent people.

"How much money you got to pay?" the old man growled.

"For bringing a doctor to the Green River, I'll pay—"

"Ain't no doctor to bring," the man said. "I know an old Injun medicine man. He's been treating snakebites, broken arms and grizzly chews for longer than you been alive, woman."

"My name is Jessie," she said. "And while I respect Indian medicine, that's not what I'm looking for."

"Suit yourself. You stayin' to eat?"

"Are you going for a doctor?" Jessie demanded.

"Nope. A medicine man or nothing, providin' the price is right."

Jessie lost her temper. "What kind of a person are you!" she said in anger. "My friend is maybe dying and all you care about is the money!"

The man looked up. "I'm glad we both understand

21

that, ma'am. I ain't no Christian and I damn sure ain't no do-gooder. Only thing I am is a man that leaves folks alone and wants to be left alone."

The man sliced off a chunk of meat and skewered it on a stout, green willow pole, then shoved it over the fire to burn and sizzle. "Now, ma'am. You kin eat or not. Go or stay. Don't matter none to me. But it's a good forty miles down to Salt Lake City and forty harder miles back up this mountain. By then, you'll know that I was tellin' you the truth about the Mormon not being willin' to help those that don't believe in the Angel of Moroni and the gold tablets and all that foofaraw."

Jessie sat down on a log. "I didn't come to argue religion. I came to save my friend's life."

"And I'm tellin' you, an Injun medicine man is his best chance. Maybe his only chance."

Jessie wanted to bury her head in her hands and weep. "What's his name?"

"Medicine Joe."

Jessie groaned. "What tribe?"

"Shoshoni."

"They're good people," Jessie said.

The man yanked the burning hunk of elk meat out of the fire and bit off a chunk. "You seem to think everybody's nice folks. The Mormons, the Shoshoni, even me. You're a trusting and a handsome woman. How much money you got?"

Jessie stood up and walked off a ways to think. She knew that making the right decision was crucial. If she erred, it might very well cost Ki his life. Some medicine men were excellent healers, but there were quacks just as there were among the white men. If this man was a quack, Ki would probably die before she could make another trip out of these mountains.

22

Jessie turned. "Does this man know the great chief Washaki?"

"Know him?" The mountain man made an expression of disgust. "Hell, he saved Washaki's life! You meet the chief, he'll tell you it's true."

"All right," Jessie sighed. "I'll pay you fifty dollars."

"And Medicine Joe? He'll be happy with twenty-five."

"No," Jessie said emphatically. "If he saves my friend's life, he gets the same as you. But if he fails, then he gets nothing."

The mountain man shook his head. "You look softer than wet buffalo dump, but you ain't, are you, pretty woman?"

"No," Jessie said. "I'm not soft at all, and if you or Medicine Joe think that I'm going to pay you and then be tricked and left with nothing, you'll be making the worst mistake of your life."

"Big words for a woman."

Jessie drew and fired her six-gun in one smooth, quick motion. Her bullet slammed into the hunk of a singed and blackened meat on the end of the man's stick and sent it flying.

"I mean what I say," she said quietly. "And you'd better do your Shoshoni friend a big favor and tell him what I said."

For the first time, the mountain man actually smiled as he regarded the bullet-shattered end of his roasting stick.

"I reckon I will," he said. "Old Medicine Joe can be a little coyote sometimes. But he sure knows how to brew up some powerful healing spirits and concotions. You just wait and see if I'm not telling you how it is for a fact."

"When can we get him and get started back to the Green River?" Jessie asked pointedly.

"Soon as you pay me the fifty dollars and I eat my fill, then I'll go fetch him in my canoe."

Jessie dug into her jeans and pulled out a wad of greenbacks. "Twenty-five dollars now, twenty-five dollars when we reach the Green River with your friend."

The man took her money with a shake of his shaggy, gray mane. "You sure aren't very trusting, are you?"

"Not when my friend's life hangs in the balance," Jessie said.

"How far away is the medicine man?"

"Other end of the lake, then about ten miles more."

"Good," Jessie said. "I'd appreciate it if you would eat faster and be on your way. I'd like to start back tonight."

The man barked a laugh. "Lady, you look plumb tuckered out to me. I reckon a little of this meat and a good night's sleep will help cure you of your suspicious nature. We'll leave at dawn."

Jessie just didn't have the strength to argue. In truth, she was at the end of her endurance. "What is your given name?"

"Moses," the man said, with a shake of his head. "My ma was a Bible thumper. My pa was a whiskey peddler and a poker player that got shot when I was but ten years old. Hated him anyway. 'Most as much as I hate my name."

Jessie took the stick out of the man's hand and motioned for him to cut her a strip of elk meat. She was too damned tired and discouraged to make conversation. All she wanted was food and sleep and then to reach Ki and help him live.

Chapter 4

The hard scraping of a frying pan against the blade of a bowie knife awakened Jessie long before daylight. She had been persuaded to sleep in the old mountain man's cabin, though the sight and smell of it had been almost as disagreeable as the thought of another nocturnal visit by a marauding grizzly bear.

"Wake up, ma'am," old Moses said, lighting his rusted-out tin stove and fueling it with pinecones until he had a crackling good fire. "We're gonna have some more elk meat and then we'll hit the trail. Gonna be a long way back to the Green River."

Jessie groaned. She felt as if she had just closed her eyes for an instant and it was already time to get up. But the thought of Ki lying alone wounded beside the Green River drove her to her feet. She needed to make her toilet so she stumbled outside and headed for the bushes.

Ten minutes later, she was bending over beside the lake, scooping big handfuls up to wash the sleep from her eyes. The stars were quickly fading, and the faint gray light of predawn was already peeking hopefully over the western horizon.

Jessie took a deep breath, wishing she had a washcloth

or something. She knew that a clean one would not be available to her in the cabin, so she braved the morning chill and removed her wool shirt. Very carefully, she soaked the sleeve she had not cut off, then wrung out the excess water and used the sleeve to scrub her face, neck and arms.

There, she thought, as the cold air and the frigid water combined to rouse her into wakefulness, much better. She turned around to glance at the cabin, and a gasp erupted from her lips as she almost bumped into an old Indian. He wore a blanket wrapped around his thin shoulders and was staring at her exposed breasts with a wide grin.

"Good tits," he said with unconcealed admiration.

Jessie turned around quickly and pulled on her now-sleeveless shirt. "Dammit, you shouldn't sneak up on people that way! Who are you, Medicine Joe?"

"Yep."

Jessie finished buttoning up her shirt and tried to hide her annoyance. She turned to face the old Indian, and the fact that he was still smiling and staring at her bosom, despite its being fully covered, did nothing to improve her humor.

"Your friend says that you once saved Chief Washaki's life. Is that true?"

"Yep."

"How?"

"Him fight bear, just like your friend," Medicine Joe said. "Bad hurt, but I heal."

Jessie frowned. She sure wanted to believe in this old Indian. "Did you bring good medicines?"

"Yep." The Indian raised a buckskin pouch up to her eyes. It was decorated with beads, and even though the light was poor, Jessie could see that it was bulging with

26

something, probably herbs, Indian charms and secret potions.

"Then let's go," Jessie said.

"Money first."

"Twenty-five dollars now, twenty-five when you heal my friend. If you don't heal him, nothing. Is that understood?"

"Yep."

"Good." Jessie gave the Indian twenty-five dollars, and he carefully counted it twice to make sure that he was not being shorted. Satisfied, he rolled the greenbacks up and stuffed them into his buckskin pouch.

"Let's eat," Jessie said, heading for the cabin.

The elk meat was tough, half-cooked, and yet it tasted wonderful. The night before, Jessie had been too tired to eat well, but this morning, as dawn was breaking color across the alpine lake, she was famished. She ate as much as both the old men combined, and when she was finished, the three of them left their dirty plates and utensils on the table and abandoned the crater.

Moses proved to be a demon of a walker and Medicine Joe was a close second. They were old but tough, and there wasn't a bit of fat on either man, only gristle, muscle and bone. They walked hard all day and far into that first night and managed to arrive at the Green River late the second night instead of the next morning as Jessie had expected.

Ki's health had deteriorated greatly. He was now drifting in and out of dreams, and sometimes the fever raged so strong in him that he babbled softly in Japanese. Jessie had to pry his jaws open to get water down his parched throat, but Ki was unable to swallow food.

When Jessie unwrapped the bandage she had made, she was shocked and greatly disheartened to see that the wound was suppurating badly and that dark, poisonous-looking blood lines were fanning out toward the samurai's heart.

"He's going to die if we don't do something fast," she said, almost choking with tears of desperation.

Medicine Joe, after studying the samurai for almost ten minutes, shook his head and also looked gloomy.

"Him very bad," the Indian said. "Evil spirits in his blood. Very bad now. Probably die soon."

"No!" Jessie cried in protest. "You *must* save him. I'll . . . I'll pay you one hundred dollars if you can make him live."

"Hey!" Moses complained. "That ain't fair you give him that much and me only half."

"Yes it is," Jessie said fretfully. "He's the one that's got to make a miracle."

Moses didn't like that, but he had to admit his role was secondary to the Shoshoni's.

With the promise of what would be a fortune to a poor Indian, Medicine Joe wasted no time in putting forth his best efforts. He had brought a pot and several tin cups, and he ordered a fire to be made and water to be heated before he disappeared into the forest.

"Where's he going!"

"To collect things," Moses snorted, still angered by the fact that he was being paid less than his old Shoshoni friend. "You know, bugs, beetles, bark, roots, leaves and the like."

Jessie fussed with the fire, and when it was burning well, she filled the Indian's pot with water to boil, then went and sponged Ki's forehead.

"He's burning up." She fretted.

"Why you so worried?" Moses asked. "He's just a Chinaman, ain't he? They sure ain't all that special."

28

Jessie's anger got the better of her. "Chinaman! You old fool, he's a *samurai*! Now I know that means nothing to you, but he's the best fighter you'll ever lay your eyes on. He can fire arrows faster, swifter and more accurately than any Indian. His hands and feet are more deadly than a war club to an Indian or a knife in the hands of the most skilled fighter."

"Hogwash!"

"It's true!"

Jessie reached into the samurai's tunic and found a *shuriken* star blade. "And this," she said, "is a star blade. He can hurl these like bullets, and I've seen him kill or wound professional gunfighters before they can even get their six-guns out of their holsters."

"Ha!"

"Laugh," Jessie said, "but it's the laugh of ignorance. Ki isn't a Chinaman, either. His father was an American seaman. A strong, brave man who went to Japan and fell in love with Ki's mother, who was born high but tragically was disowned because she married one of our race."

"What the hell for!"

"It may surprise you, Moses, but the Japanese and the Chinese—to name two ancient Oriental races—consider us their inferiors in every respect."

"Inferiors!" Moses ranted. "Why, we are bigger and stronger, tougher and smarter than they'll ever be."

"We may be a larger race, but the rest of what you claim is unsupported," Jessie said.

"By God, that's ripe!"

"Listen," she said, "from what I hear, the Chinese are making a mark in the Sierras. They're proving themselves to be both tough and strong. They don't quit when things get rough, and as for being smarter, we

29

are the nation with very little historical culture. Theirs goes back unknown centuries."

Moses shook his head. "I don't know what you're getting so het up about—defendin' the Celestials against your own kind. But if this Ki fella is half-white, how come he wears his hair in a damn pigtail and is dressed in that funny Chinaman costume?"

"It's the uniform of the samurai," Jessie said, wishing that Medicine Joe would return. Arguing or trying to explain things to this old man was probably a waste of time and breath, but since there was nothing else to do, she continued.

"A samurai is trained from his earliest childhood to serve a master, and he is willing to give his life—without hesitation—toward that end."

"Humph."

"Well," Jessie snapped, "you can 'humph' and snicker if you want, but Ki has risked his life dozens of times for me. And when he is not doing that, he keeps his mind and his body trained, using the strictest of discipline and constant practice. The proof of what I'm telling you lies in that campfire. My samurai friend killed that grizzly with his knife."

Moses had already looked over the dead, half-charred grizzly lying in the fire ring. "That's a hell of a big bear. But I saw the hole where he was shot. Wasn't no knife that did it."

"Look again," Jessie said. "I shot him with my Winchester, but Ki had already administered the death blows with his knife. If you don't believe me, roll the beast onto his back and take a look at his stomach, where you'll find Ki's knife still buried to the hilt."

Moses did just that, though he really had a struggle. "Here it is," he said, pulling the samurai's *tanto* blade

30

out of the belly of the bear. He came back and handed it to Jessie. The handle was burned, but the blade had been protected by the bear's body and was unmarked.

Jessie slipped the knife into Ki's pack, knowing that the samurai would repair the handle and that the quality of the steel was the thing that was most important.

Medicine Joe returned with a second pouch stuffed with all manner of things. He asked both Jessie and Moses to go away while he mixed his secret potions and medicines, and when they protested, the Indian folded his arms across his chest and refused to budge until his wishes were granted.

"Damned superstitious old fart!" Moses raged.

Jessie was equally angered but not enough to lose sight of the fact that everything depended on Medicine Joe's skills.

She and Moses went over to look at the first horse that had been killed by the grizzly, and after studying it for a few minutes, Moses said, "You sure ran into two big ones, ma'am. It's a wonder that you're still alive."

"I wouldn't be if it wasn't for Ki. He pushed me aside from the bear's charge and met the beast head-on."

Moses was silent for a few minutes before he cleared his throat and said, "I reckon I spoke out of turn a while ago about your friend. A brave man is a brave man, no matter what his color or station in life. I sure hope he lives, and it ain't got nothing to do with your money."

"Thanks," Jessie said quietly. "Ki is the kind of man that you like to ride the trail with. He's the kind that you'd also like to have beside you whenever there is trouble."

Jessie reached out and squeezed the mountain man's buckskin-clad arm. "I suspect you're that kind of man too, Moses."

31

The old mountain man swelled up a little in the chest at those words, and his eyes burned a little brighter. "Well," he said. "You're the kind of woman that a man would like to bed and even wed."

Before Jessie could recover from that strange but heartfelt compliment, Medicine Joe called her to come back to the fire and help.

He made her stir the pot while he sprinkled his herbs, leaves, roots, and even wildflowers into it until they were as thick as mash. Then, when the mixture was smoking and bubbling, the Indian lifted the scorched pot barehanded out of the fire.

"What are you going to do, feed him this stuff?" Jessie asked with growing alarm.

Medicine Joe ignored her question until he had ladled up a big spoonful. Jessie grabbed his wrist. "He'll choke to death on it. He can't swallow!"

In answer, the Shoshoni turned the ladle over, and the dark, steaming mixture dropped into Ki's terribly infected wound. The samurai's body stiffened, his lips drew back from his teeth in agony and he moaned.

"What are you doing? You're burning his flesh!"

Jessie started to grab the ladle, but the Indian looked up at Moses, and the old man pinned her arms and hissed, "I've watched this before. It's rough, but it's the only thing that will do to draw out the poison. Better his flesh burns than corrupts. Better he suffers than dies. Eh, Miss Jessie?"

Jessie closed her eyes and fought for self-control. "Yes," she whispered hoarsely. "You can let go of me now."

"You sure?"

She nodded, and Moses released her from his powerful grip. Jessie sat on her hands and watched as the Shoshoni

Indian, face streaming with perspiration that dripped onto Ki's chest, kept ladling the boiling mass onto Ki's shoulder and then using the ladle to spread it out across the dark poison lines that were expanding like tentacles across his bare chest.

"It'll either cure him . . . or kill him with the next four hours," Moses explained in a gentle voice. "One or the other."

Jessie swallowed and fought back tears. She could not bear to watch Ki convulse powerfully with each searing application of the poultice, so she turned away and busied herself with breaking up little sticks to add to the fire.

Medicine Joe began to chant, softly at first, then louder and stronger.

Four hours, Jessie thought. For Ki, that might be a lifetime.

Chapter 5

Ki survived the crucial four hours, and his fever broke ten hours after Medicine Joe began to force a vile-looking drink down his throat. Within three days, the samurai was sitting up and eating.

Watching him closely, Jessie saw that he was in considerable discomfort whenever he moved. "How many ribs did the grizzly break?" she asked quietly.

"Who said they were broken?"

"You don't have to say it," Jessie told him. "Even a samurai shows pain, if one knows how to read the signs. So how many?"

"Three, maybe four of the lower on the right side. But they'll heal very fast."

"I know that," Jessie said. She stood up and walked out of the camp to join Moses and Medicine Joe.

"Here's the rest of your hundred dollars," Jessie said, handing it to the Shoshoni medicine man. "I can't tell you how grateful we are for your help. You performed a miracle."

"Yep," Medicine Joe said, rolling up the greenbacks and poking them into his buckskin pouch.

"And Moses," Jessie added, turning to the strong old mountain man, "we are on our way to the Sierra Nevadas. If you'd like to help us reach them, there's more money in it for you."

"Why you wanna go there?" Moses asked with a shake of his head. "You won't find nothin' in those mountains that's as good as what you'll find in the Wasatch or the Rockies. Hell, even the Wind River Mountains are full of game and—"

"We're going to help them build a railroad over the Sierras," Jessie interrupted.

"A railroad! What the hell would you wanna do a dumb thing like that for?"

Jessie had grown accustomed to the man's insults, which were not meant to be personal. "It's not us. There are a group of investors they call the Big Four. Charles Crocker, Leland Stanford, Collis Huntington and Mark Hopkins."

"Never heard of a one of them." Moses groused. "Must be a pack of rich fools."

Jessie tried to explain about the transcontinental railroad, and this was a mistake because it only upset the mountain man.

"You mean they are going to drive rails over these Wasatch Mountains too!"

"Not close to your lake," Jessie said, eager to reassure the man. "But yes, it will link with the Sierra railroad and join Sacramento, California, to the Missouri River."

"Jesus have mercy on us!" Moses cried. "This country is gonna be overrun with pilgrims trying to dig up the ground, plant things and generally muck it all up."

"It will bring more settlers," Jessie said. "I won't try to tell you otherwise. But this country begs for families

35

and towns. Back in the East, they are living on top of each other in the big cities."

"The hell with 'em," Moses growled. "Just because they've ruined things back there don't mean they got to come to the West and do it all over again."

Jessie expelled a deep breath. "There are good people who need opportunity, and the railroad will open up the West for them. I can understand how you feel, but I believe this nation has to be bound together, and a transcontinental railroad seems to be the only thing that can do it."

Moses toed the dirt with his moccasin and frowned. Without meeting Jessie's eyes, he muttered, "How much money is in helping you and your samurai across Paiute country? Them Indians is as likely as not to catch and scalp the lot of us."

"I'll pay you five hundred dollars to get us safely to Donner Pass."

Moses swallowed noisily, and his eyes lit up with excitement. "That's a heap of money!"

"It is," Jessie said. "But as you said, the risks are high."

"I fought the Paiute before," Mose said. "I don't like 'em much."

"I'm going to do all I can to avoid them," Jessie said. "A railroad is coming through their lands, and I'm sure not going to make building it any more dangerous than it already will be for the advance crews. To get through without being seen, I'll need your help, Moses."

"Okay," the man said, "seein' as how I'm probably the only white man alive can get you across the Nevada Territory without getting your scalps razed. But what about your friend? He sure ain't fit to travel."

"Where we go, he goes," Jessie said flatly. "That's

the way of it even if I have to take him to California by myself."

"You sure are a stubborn woman," Moses complained. "The only way it would work is if we get ourselves horses. A couple for us to ride and another one to pull along a travois with your friend strapped on it tight."

"I agree," Jessie said. "Can you find us horses?"

"I reckon. But draggin' along a travois is going to make things a whole lot more difficult."

Jessie glanced back at the camp to see Ki before she lowered her voice and said, "Moses, you saw what he did to that bear even as it was tearing his shoulder open. Think about it. We may have to go a lot slower, but the samurai will always stand ready to fight. If we run into trouble, you'll be glad he's with us, even if he is still flat on his back."

"Maybe," Moses said skeptically, "but a travois will leave a trail that can't be hid. We'd just be tellin' the Paiute that we was wounded and ready to be took."

"Ki is my best friend," Jessie said, putting it another way. "I guess you wouldn't leave your best friend behind, would you?"

"No," Moses said with great reluctance. "I reckon not. All right then, I'll do it."

"Good," Jessie said.

She walked back to rejoin Ki. "We'll be leaving soon. Moses believes he can find horses. Once we have them we can make a travois for you and—"

"No," Ki said. "We don't need horses on my account. I can walk."

"Don't be ridiculous. You've lost too much blood and you're still much too weak. I want you to conserve your energy and regain your strength. I'll be counting on you when we reach the deserts of Nevada."

37

Ki was silent for several moments before he said, "If Moses can get horses, I'll ride, not be dragged along behind. Lying on a travois being pulled over mountainous country would almost certainly result in tearing my shoulder wound open again. Besides, riding would be much faster."

"Agreed," Jessie said as Moses and the Shoshoni came over to join them. "So all we have to do is find horses."

Moses said, "Be no problem, ma'am. If you've got cash money, Medicine Joe and I can find a few Injun ponies to buy. Just rest easy, and we ought to be back with ponies in a day or two."

Jessie hesitated, and Ki said, "Why don't you and Moses go and leave Medicine Joe here with me?"

Jessie liked that arrangement much better. It wasn't that she was certain Moses and the Shoshoni would take her horse-buying money and leave her stranded, but it was a possibility that had to be considered. "Are you sure that will be all right?"

Ki nodded. "Of course. Medicine Joe can keep boiling his poultices and making me drink his awful brews. In a couple more days, I'll be much stronger."

"All right then," Jessie said. "That's what we'll do."

"Aw, ma'am! I sure wish you'd stay here and let Joe and me go find them horses. Might be dangerous."

"I'm going with you," Jessie said with determination. "And you might just as well get used to the idea."

Moses wasn't pleased. In fact, he was downright angry from the looks of him, but Jessie didn't care. "There is no sense in waiting. Let's leave now," she said.

Moses grabbed his rifle and a leather "possibles bag" that he carried and in which he collected all manner of things. "Let's save our breath for the walkin'," he said shortly. "You just better be able to keep up."

"I will," Jessie snapped, feeling insulted.

Angry and perverse, Moses struck off on the trail walking like a demon. It was all Jessie could do to keep up with his long strides, and her own anger fed her determination as they followed the Green River south. Moses didn't stop until the sun went down.

They had a silent, sullen camp and left before dawn. The old mountain man tried to resume his former pace, but he was as tired as Jessie, and when he could not make her beg for him to slow down, he grew weary of attempting to teach her a lesson and finally began to ease up his pace.

"Where are we going?" Jessie asked. "I thought that we'd be going north to find the Shoshoni."

"It'd take us a week to reach their Wind River Valley," Moses said. "But just another day's hike is another huge valley where the Indians like to spend their summer hunting. Last time I was there, they even had a few buffalo they kept hidden from the white hunters."

"I see," Jessie said, realizing that Moses had chosen to gamble.

Late that evening, they spotted fresh Indian pony tracks. Moses studied them carefully and then pointed south. "I reckon we'll find them camped in that valley I told you about."

Jessie said nothing but followed the man until darkness made further progress impossible. They made a cold camp that night and again ate jerked elk, then rolled up in their blankets and went to sleep.

Jessie awoke to the sound of running hoofbeats. She jumped to her feet, reaching for her six-gun while still half-asleep. She saw Moses on horseback, galloping into camp driving about ten Indian ponies.

"What's going on?"

"Ute!" the old man hollered. "I had a bad feeling yesterday, and so I went huntin' 'em up just to make sure we didn't stumble onto the wrong damn Indians tomorrow morning. Good thing, too!"

"But . . . but why'd you steal their horses?"

"Are we going to stand her and palaver until the Ute catch up with us and roast our bones for breakfast!"

"No," Jessie said, reaching for one of the Indian ponies, which had a braided leather rope tied around its neck. "I guess not. But you were supposed to *buy* us horses! I thought we had an understanding."

"Sure we did," Moses said, kicking his pony north, "but the Ute and me don't see eye to eye on anything. Fact is, they'd kill me on sight. You see, I been feudin' with 'em for near twenty years."

"Damn!" Jessie swore. "If I'd have known that, then I'd have gone in to bargain with them myself."

"And they'd have had your pretty hair hanging on a war lance. Them people just don't like white folks."

Jessie fumed, but since there was no possible way to undo the damage, she knew that the only thing left to do was to drive the ponies north, reach Ki and Medicine Joe and put as much distance between themselves and the Ute as possible.

She and Moses returned to the camp on the Green River in eight hours on horseback, covering the same distance it had taken them two days to walk.

Not once did they see any sign of pursuit, although it was sure to come once the Indians found themselves replacement mounts. The Ute were famous as horse-thieves and were expert riders. They were not the kind of people you wanted to dog your backtrail.

Medicine Joe and Ki saw them an hour before they arrived, driving the band of ponies up the Green River.

By the time they reached camp, Ki and the Shoshoni were on their feet and had everything ready to pack and leave.

"We got big troubles," Moses said.

"Damn Utes again," Medicine Joe growled. "You supposed to go north, not south!"

"There's no time for this," Jessie said.

Ki said not a word. One look at the lathered Ute ponies told him everything.

Jessie took only enough time to bind the samurai's broken ribs as tightly as possible. Because of them, Ki had to climb onto a rock to get mounted. However, once on horseback, he lifted his chin and gave every indication that he was ready and able to keep up with the three of them.

"Let's get out of here!" Moses said, his eyes jerking to his backtrail every few seconds. "I think this was all their horses, but if it wasn't, they'll be coming even if it's only one or two. They won't stop comin' either, not until we get over the Wasatch."

"What about you, Medicine Joe?" Jessie asked.

"I never seen Sierras before," the Indian said. "Maybe this good time."

Jessie and Ki exchanged questioning glances, but there was no time for conversation. Jessie knew that Moses was right when he said that if even one Indian could find a horse and pursue them, he would do so and be more than willing to risk his life for the high honor of returning his hunting party's band of ponies.

That meant that they'd be constantly looking over their shoulders for the next hundred miles or more.

Chapter 6

As Jessie stood on a high mountain, she knew the Utes were somewhere far behind them, probably still trying desperately to overtake her party before they reached the safety of Salt Lake City. Well, Jessie thought, they have failed.

She was still irritated about the Ute ponies and the dangerous predicament Moses had placed them all in by his thievery.

"Turn the extra ponies loose," she said.

"What!" Moses exploded in anger. "Now you can't be serious."

"I am very serious. Turn them loose."

"But hell fire!" Moses shouted. "If they'd stole ours they sure as hell not turn 'em back to us. I can probably get fifteen, twenty dollars a head for them from the Mormons."

"Turn 'em loose," Jessie repeated once more.

Moses swore and fussed, but in the end, he accepted Jessie's orders, and the Ute ponies they did not need to ride were turned away.

Before they started down from the Wasatch, Jessie cast a worried glance at the samurai. "Are you all right?"

Ki nodded.

"When we get to town, we'll find a doctor," Jessie promised.

But Ki shook his head. "There's no need for that," he told her. "Medicine Joe did his job very well. The wound is healing clean. It's just going to take a little time."

The Shoshoni overheard Ki's comment, and he swelled up a little with pride. "Indian medicine good," he grunted.

"It is," Ki said. "It saved my life."

"How are the ribs?" Jessie asked.

"They're getting better every day," Ki said. He remounted and signaled that he was ready to go on.

Jessie studied the huge basin before them. The Great Salt Lake shimmered in the heat waves, and she could see miles of salt flats ringing the still body of water. There were also thousands of acres of green fields, all as neatly blocked and spaced as a checkerboard.

"They've turned a desert into an oasis," she said to herself and the others. "It makes you realize that all it takes to make the roughest western land bloom is water and work."

"They're hell for workin', all right," Moses grunted. "I never said them people were lazy—just wrong and stubborn as blind mules."

"They're following their own beliefs," Jessie said. "They ought to be left alone."

In reply, Moses whipped his pony down a steep trail. For the next four difficult hours, they followed a series of sharp switchbacks down the mountainside. Their trail brought them to a point about three miles south of Salt Lake City itself, and they followed a dusty road past neat farms and ranches. Jessie saw women washing and hang-

43

ing clothes, and happy, healthy children playing in the yards and fields.

Because they were strangers riding Indian ponies, they attracted much attention. Even farm dogs came to bark at them with excitement, and people stopped their work to stare at them as they passed. But whenever Jessie waved, they waved in return.

Many terrible things had been written about these people, but it gave Jessie a good feeling to see them finally settled in their own Deseret, no longer ridiculed and persecuted for their religious beliefs. Witnessing their prospering and turning desert into productive ranch and farmland simply reinforced her own opinion that the West was plenty big enough to accommodate all kinds of people. White, Indian, Chinese and all religions.

They approached a big horse ranch just south of town and saw a tall, handsome man working a stallion on a lead line. The stallion was an Appaloosa, and its spots made a striking "blanket" across its hindquarters.

When the man saw them riding the little Indian ponies bareback, he stopped his work, patted the stallion affectionately before turning it into a corral, then came over to greet them.

"Hello there," he called.

"Ignore him," Moses growled.

But Jessie had her own ideas. She was not going to spend any time in Salt Lake City, but that didn't mean they wouldn't need some fresh supplies and food for the long journey they still faced across Utah and Nevada. This young man looked helpful and friendly, and Jessie was determined to seek his company and find out if he could tell them where they could buy supplies and maybe even some better horses and real saddles.

44

The man stepped between the corral poles and pushed back his hat. He was broad-shouldered and freckle-faced. His lips were cracked, but his eyes were friendly and he had a trusting face.

"Howdy," he said. "I see you're riding Indian ponies. Going far?"

"Might be," Moses said, his voice rough and unfriendly. "But it ain't none of your concern."

The man's smile slipped until Jessie hastily added, "You have a nice horse ranch and that Appaloosa stallion is beautiful."

The man was pleased at the compliment. "Thank you. He's the only horse on the place that I own. The rest belong to my brother."

"Well," Jessie said, "he's a fine animal. I'm afraid we can't quite say the same thing about these Indian ponies, though they've gotten us here safely."

The man's eyes brushed over the ponies, and he seemed to gauge them all in a single glance. "They're plenty run down," he said. "Look like they've been used hard."

"They have," Jessie said. "I'd be interested in buying some fresh horses. Saddles and bridles too."

The man beamed. "Well you sure came to the right place. I'm a horse trainer and so is my brother. We both make saddles on the side to help out during the lean times. Why don't you come on up to the house? I can show you some things you might be interested in."

"We'll do that," Jessie said, liking the man and extremely eager to ride a saddle instead of the sharp, knobby backbone of an skinny Indian pony.

The man managed to take his eyes off Jessie and the Ute ponies long enough to notice that Ki was heavily bandaged. "Say, you've been hurt! Why, here I am

45

shooting the breeze and you're in pain. There's a doctor that lives about three miles down the road. I'll—"

"Thank you anyway," Ki said. "But Medicine Joe here is taking care of things."

"But we could certainly use fresh horses, saddles and bridles," Jessie said. "We've been riding mountain country and it's no fun bareback."

"Might be you want a little liniment too." Suddenly, the young man blushed, realizing what he'd said. "I . . . I meant no offense, ma'am."

"None taken," Jessie told him with a smile.

Their eyes met, and their gazes lingered intimately for a few moments. Jessie felt her cheeks warm. For a Mormon, this handsome young man had a very bold look about him.

"Have you owned this ranch long?" she asked.

"Oh," he said quickly. "It isn't mine. I'm not even Mormon. I'm just here to help my brother. He's Mormon, but he busted both his legs when a horse reared up and went over backward on him this spring. He asked me to come out from Colorado and help him until he's back on his feet."

"I see," Jessie said. "That was nice of you."

The man shrugged. "My name is Frank Palmer. My brother's name is Ollie, only he isn't here right now. But I know he'd want me to help you out. And . . . well, we could use a little extra cash."

Now that Moses had learned that Frank wasn't a Mormon, he became more civil. "These Indian ponies, they're worth a lot more than a man might first think," he said. "They're tough little buggers. Take a man a long, long way."

Frank nodded. "Oh, they're tough. Mustangs always are. But they're too small for tall men like us. And they're

46

too undersized for the heavy work of pulling plow. If they're gentle, I can make them into good children's ponies. But that's about all they're good for."

Jessie said nothing until they reached the ranch house. She wearily dismounted, and the insides of her legs were hot from the long, sweaty hours she'd spent on the back of the horse.

The ranch house was small but neat, and off to one side was a pond with ducks and geese. Besides the many horses she saw in the corrals, there was a barn, a well and a very well-stocked shed where an anvil and forge stood ready to use.

Frank was showing them around. "If you buy horses from me or my brother, we shoe 'em fresh and we do it right. We'd never want it said that the Palmer men had a customer ride off only to throw a shoe a few miles down the road. No sir! We sell sound horses at fair prices. But first, we're going to feed you folks and then we can talk business."

Jessie and her friends were too starved to put up even a token argument. Soon, Frank had a table filled with bread, butter, milk and thick slices of roast beef. Moses and Medicine Joe ate like desperate men, and Jessie and Ki did not hold back.

When the meal was over, Moses and Medicine Joe found a shady spot to nap in under a tree. Since walking was painful to his ribs, Ki also rested, while Jessie and Frank went out to look at horses and saddles.

"Now," Frank said, taking her to a corral, "those four horses over there are the best I have to offer right now. They are all sound, and none of them are over seven years old."

Jessie was an excellent judge of horseflesh. Three of the animals that Frank pointed out looked to be strong

47

and fast, but the fourth, a sorrel gelding, was not straight-legged enough to suit her.

"I'll take them except for the sorrel—if the price is right," she added.

Frank nodded with a look of approval. "You've a good eye, all right. How far you going?"

"All the way to Donner Pass."

Frank blinked and his smile faded. "Sure wish you'd change your mind about that. The Paiute are raiding between here and Reno."

"We'll just have to take our chances."

Frank was silent for several minutes. "The three horses you picked are all fast, and they've got the endurance you'll need to outrun and stay ahead of Indians. But. . . ."

Jessie waited for a moment, then said, "But what?"

"Well, a young, beautiful woman like you ought to have a special kind of horse. One that would get her out of any kind of Indian trouble. The thought of a woman like you being captured and used gives me a cold knot in the stomach."

"It doesn't do anything for me either," Jessie said, "but I don't see such an animal here."

"Might be I'd let you have that Appaloosa stallion," Frank said quietly.

"Really! I'd love to have him. But I had the feeling that you and that horse were pretty special friends."

"We are. I raised him from a colt. Best horse I ever owned."

"Then I couldn't buy him from you," Jessie said. "It wouldn't be right."

"Okay," Frank said, "then I'll loan him to you."

Jessie was touched by this man's generosity. He didn't know her and yet was willing to trust her with his prized horse.

"I can't promise I'll be back this way very soon."

"I know that. But it would make you return sometime. That's the important thing to me."

Frank studied her face. "Come on into the barn. I'll show you our saddles, and you can pick out four that you like."

Jessie followed him inside the barn. It was dim and cool. The scent of fresh hay filled her nostrils. He led her over to a corner of the barn under a window where the light was better. She saw at least ten saddles, several of them in a state of being built or repaired.

"These four are the ones I'd recommend," he said, moving over to the saddles and tipping each one back to show her that their fleece was in good shape.

Jessie made a show of inspecting them though she could tell at once that they were well used but in excellent condition. Most important, of course, were the latigo, the cinches and the stirrup leathers, any one of which failing in a crisis would result in a nasty fall and quite possibly death.

Satisfied, she looked up at the young horse trainer and said, "How much for them?"

"A hundred dollars for the four. Thirty dollars each for the three saddle horses and nothing for the loan of my Appaloosa."

It was a very generous price. Jessie had expected double, given the difficult circumstances.

"I'd have to pay you a fair price for the Appaloosa," she said. "You can buy him back for the same price. But in case something should happen to me or him on the trail to California, then. . . ."

Jessie didn't quite finish as Frank took her into his strong arms and said, "The reason I want you to have that horse is so that nothing will happen to you."

49

"And that's important to you? Why?"

He shrugged and smiled down at her face. "Because you are the most beautiful woman I've ever seen."

Jessie closed her eyes and her lips found Frank's. Their kisses flamed her passions, and he pulled her down onto the bed of clean straw. When he began to unbutton her blouse, she whispered, "I can't believe this is happening so suddenly."

"You're in a hurry," he said, "so there's no choice, is there?"

Jessie slipped out of her shirt, and he fell upon her breasts like a hungry animal. She groaned and reached down to unbuckle his pants.

A moment later, he was undressing her completely, and they were moving against each other, breath coming fast, hands, lips and tongues exploring, creating wonderful sensations.

"Your breasts drive me wild," he panted, pushing her thighs wide apart and moving between them.

Jessie's hand stroked his manhood until it was long and hard. "I'll still have to pay you for the Appaloosa," she whispered.

"This is payment enough," he said, his voice hoarse with desire as his narrow rider's hips thrust forward until she gasped with pleasure and felt herself being opened like the petals of a flower.

Jessie's fingernails kneaded his buttocks, and when he slipped into her hot wetness, she sighed with happiness.

"This is the very last thing I was expecting when we rode in here on those Indian ponies."

"Any regrets?"

She laughed deep in her throat as his body filled her completely. "No, not yet."

Frank played her like an instrument. He was big and surprisingly experienced for a man so young. He brought her to a point of ecstasy where Jessie thought she would burst, then he slowed his hard thrusting and left her tingling with desire.

"Come on," she pleaded, "take me!"

"I will," he said. "But when I'm ready."

Jessie wasn't about to beg, so she wrapped her legs around his waist, then began to pump with all her might.

"Oh," he moaned, "I can see that you intend to take me in a hurry."

She was biting his neck and clawing his back as her body milked him into a frenzy. She thought she would go crazy until, suddenly, a deep sob escaped from her throat and she lost control. Her legs clenched his thrusting hips, and she felt his hot seed filling her as his body convulsed in a series of powerful lunges.

It was over in a long, shuddering moment, and it was good. They lay in the clean straw and slowly regained their breath.

"They'd never believe I was in here doing this," Jessie said with a chuckle.

"We don't care," he said, kissing her mouth, neck and ears. "Just as long as you bring my horse back safe, and we have more time together."

Jessie snuggled tight against him. "You've got a deal," she whispered. "But I think we could spend another hour like this if you'd like."

He raised himself up on his elbows and looked down at her. "I'd like very much," he said before his tongue traced a circle around her nipples and made them as stiff and inviting as chocolate drops.

Two hours later, when Jessie was mounted on the Appaloosa, Moses couldn't help but blurt, "Well, goddamn! You got twice as much horse as the rest of us!"

Frank, overhearing this remark, said, "And she's twice as pretty."

Moses snorted, Medicine Joe said nothing and Ki looked at his master and friend and noted with more than casual interest the sticks of straw in her mussed hair.

Frank touched Jessie on the thigh and said, "Just be careful. This horse will outrun and outlast anything you come across on four legs out there in those deserts. He's got a nice soft mouth and a big heart."

"So do you," Jessie whispered for his ears alone.

Mounted on such a good animal and with a fine saddle to cushion the miles they faced, Jessie now felt much more optimistic about their chances of reaching California.

"I'll bring him back," she promised. "By the way, what's his name?"

"Ranger," Frank said. "I call him Ranger."

Jessie waved good-bye and touched her heels to the stallion. The powerful Appaloosa stepped into a brisk walk as she reined him south, around the lower end of the Great Salt Lake and out toward the deserts beyond.

Chapter 7

Jessie and Ki knew that it was over a thousand miles as the crow flies to the Sierras, and that much of the way was hard, arid country. Still, Jessie was sure that they could make the trip in two weeks if they did not run into trouble. Frank had insisted that they take large skin water bags, and since all four horses had just been shod, nothing more could be done to insure their safe passage across the wastelands of Utah and Nevada.

The first night out, they camped in a ravine and hobbled their horses. Moses and Medicine Joe went right to sleep, but Ki and Jessie sat up late, talking quietly about what they expected to find when they reached the Sierras, with hope that their long trek westward would be uneventful.

"Frank said that the Paiute expected white travelers to follow the Humboldt River across Nevada," Jessie confided. "That's why he suggested that we swing north and cross over the Ruby Mountains, then strike directly west."

"What about water?" Ki asked.

"He says that the Rubys are our next sure source. I'm afraid that they are still over two hundred miles to our west."

"Any rivers between there and here?"

"No, but there are a few springs. Frank has been mustanging out this way in better times, when the Paiute weren't so upset. He says that we can follow the mustang trails and find most of those springs."

Ki looked closely at her. "You're putting your life at risk."

"I know that, but Frank wouldn't lie to me. He admitted that his recommendation to avoid the Humboldt had its drawbacks. Despite that, he still considered it the best. Moses isn't too happy about it, but he knows that Frank's reasoning makes good sense."

"Has Medicine Joe said anything?"

"No." Jessie walked over to the samurai. "What's the matter? Do you think we are making a mistake?"

"Only time will tell," Ki said. "But we'll make it to the Sierras. I'm sure of it."

Ki looked out at the desert. Somewhere in the night, a mournful coyote was yipping at the stars; a warm breeze was blowing clouds across the face of a grinning moon.

"How is the shoulder?" Jessie asked.

Ki raised his left arm and made an easy rowing motion. "It's feeling better every day," he said. "I'm not ready to take on another grizzly, but I think I could handle my bow and arrows if necessary."

"Let's just hope it won't be necessary. What about your ribs?"

"As long as I keep them bound up pretty tight, they feel fine. I'm starting be able to twist and turn without much pain."

"Don't hurry it," Jessie warned as she lay down on her saddle blankets and gazed up at the stars. "Aren't you going to go to sleep?"

"In a while," Ki said.

The samurai waited until he was sure that Jessie and the others were sound asleep, and then he slipped quietly out of the ravine, leaving the camp behind. The desert was still hot, but not uncomfortably so, and he walked briskly to the west, eager to get some badly needed exercise.

After a mile, Ki felt loosened up and began to jog. He followed a low ridge that curved off to the south, and when he had run almost three miles, he stopped and came back, moving a little stiffly because of his ribs, but still with surprising ease.

When he returned to camp, the samurai stripped off his shirt and assumed the lotus position on his blanket. He faced the moon and meditated on all the good things in his life and how important it was that he quickly regain his physical capabilities so that he would be ready if the path they were following led them into a fight with the Paiute.

They rode out before dawn the next morning, and for the next two days, they suffered the heat, blowing sand and complete absence of water. They finally saw the Ruby Mountains on the fourth day out of Salt Lake, but it was not until the sixth day that they reached the mountains and slaked their desperate thirst, then refilled their empty skin bags.

The horses that Frank Palmer had sold them lived up to their billing, but they had lost several hundred pounds in the desert crossing; even Ranger was struggling by the time they made their first good camp.

Jessie knew that the Ruby Mountains marked almost the halfway point but that the next five hundred miles were going to be more dangerous because they were entering the stronghold of the Paiute.

Because their Utah horses were so exhausted by the desert crossing, they spent two days camping beside a nice stream and allowing them all a good rest.

Moses said, "From now until we reach the Sierras, it would be best if we traveled at night."

"All right," Jessie said. "We'll fill the skin bags and our canteens with all the water we can carry, and we'll leave when the sun goes down."

That evening, they prepared carefully. So far, they'd seen nothing but a small band of mustangs the previous afternoon. The stallion, a scarred but powerful buckskin, had scented their horses and come to investigate. He'd trumpeted a challenge to Ranger to come and fight, but Jessie had tied the big Appaloosa securely to a piñon pine tree, and the wild stud soon lost interest and drove his band of tired mares off to the south.

The first night's journey across the desert passed uneventfully. Ki demonstrated his rapid recuperation by alternately walking and riding. Moses thought this was idiocy and that the samurai had suffered sunstroke, but Jessie knew that Ki was doggedly forcing his body back into perfect physical condition.

"This would make a good camp," Moses said just before dawn, when they found a low sagebrushy meadow. "I got a feeling that Paiute are crawling all over these hills." He looked to his Indian friend. "What do you think, Joe?"

The Shoshoni lifted his face to the wind and turned his head one way and then the other. He appeared tired and very grave. Medicine Joe had not spoken three words since leaving the Wasatch Mountains. Jessie had a feeling that he very much regretted his decision to see the Sierras.

"Joe?" Moses said gruffly. "Dammit, what do you

think? Are there Indians close about?"

"Yep," the Shoshoni said. "Plenty close."

Without another word, they unsaddled and watered the horses before stringing a picket line and making sure it was tied very securely.

But even after they had eaten a little jerky and taken a few swallows of warm water from their canteens, Moses was restless. He paced back and forth as daybreak was rising and when the sun was completely off the ground.

"I can't stand waitin' around without any notion of where trouble might come from," he growled. "Joe, you want to come take a look-see with me?"

"Better stay here," the Indian warned.

"Nope," Moses said. "I can feel the hair on the back of my neck risin' by the minute. If there are Paiute hereabouts, they're probably gonna chance across the tracks we made last night. I'd rather see them before they see me."

Jessie looked to Ki. His opinion was the most important. The samurai regarded the old mountain man. "Which direction do you feel them?"

"That way," Moses said, pointing to the north. "And not very far either. I think I can even smell their campfire."

Ki inhaled deeply, and he thought that the old man was right. If he was, they needed to put some distance between themselves and the Paiute rather than remain stationary until evening.

Without a word, Moses grabbed up his rifle and started north. Just as silently, Ki gathered his bow and arrows and followed the mountain man, overtaking and matching his pace as they hiked over the dry hills, careful not to step on a rattlesnake or turn a rock that would make a loud sound.

57

In less than ten minutes, Ki could smell meat cooking and taste smoke in his nostrils.

Moses was a veteran Indian fighter, and the samurai allowed the older man to remain in the lead. When they drew near enough to overhear the sound of voices, both men dropped to the earth and crawled through the sage until they reached the crest of a low hill and peered down onto the camp.

They counted twenty-four Paiute warriors. Most of them were gathered about their campfire, roasting an antelope and talking in low voices. Ki saw that many of them wore army uniforms, which he supposed they had obtained from the bodies of dead soldiers they had slain and scalped.

Moses stared down at them grim-faced and silent. After a quarter hour, he started to edge back and retreat from the camp, but suddenly, two scouts came whipping their ponies into the places all excited about something.

Ki concentrated on their words, but he did not understand until Moses leaned very close and whispered, "We're in big trouble now. Them two boys found our horseshoe tracks about three or four miles back."

Even as he was speaking, Paiute warriors were snatching up their weapons—some only had bows and arrows, but many had good carbines. A big Indian with a knife-scarred face and a yellow bandana around his head seemed to take command, and within minutes, two of the Indians were ordered to guard the camp while the rest hurried to their ponies. They galloped out of the camp, following the leader, and their dust hung motionless in the still morning air.

Now Moses edged back and his face was pale. "They'll be finding those tracks and following 'em to camp. We'll never make it back in time!"

Ki listened to the drumming beat of the Indian ponies as they raced away. "I'll make it," he vowed. "You wait here, and we'll bring the horses on the run."

Moses opened his mouth to protest but closed it, knowing that it was the only chance they had left. If Ki failed to reach Jessie and Medicine Joe first, it was the end of the line for all of them. The Shoshoni and the woman would be overrun, then killed or captured. The Paiute would show no mercy to them if they could take them alive. Jessie would be raped by every man and then beaten, perhaps to death; the Shoshoni would be horribly tortured to test his bravery and then slaughtered.

"I'll have to kill those three guards," Moses said. "There ain't no help for it."

Ki nodded. The old man was right. Both of them would have their own job to do and do well if they were to have any chance of surviving long enough to race across the badlands of eastern and central Nevada.

Chapter 8

Ki started out running easily, until his body and muscles loosened, and then he accelerated across the desert. His shoulder felt good, but his ribs were still very tender, and whenever he had to jump a rock or a bush, he grunted softly with pain.

Ki did not know how long it would take the mounted Paiute to find Jessie and Medicine Joe, but he reckoned it would take him less than a quarter of an hour to reach the camp. Another three or four minutes would be necessary to catch and saddle the horses. It was also critical that they have a few moments to lash the water-filled bags to the saddles before they tried to make it a horse race.

Everything depended on reaching Jessie and the Shoshoni in time to get the horses saddled, loaded and mounted before the Paiute arrived in camp.

Ki's heart began to pound in his ears after a mile of hard running, and the sound of it almost masked the ominous warning of a rattlesnake that lay coiled in his path. Ki saw it only at the very last moment, and when it stuck, all he could do was hurl himself upward. The reptile's fangs caught empty air as Ki sailed over its head, landed running and never looked back.

"Jessie!" he shouted when he was still a good half mile away from their camp. "The Paiute are coming. Saddle the horses!"

Jessie and Medicine Joe both heard the warning and, most likely, so did the Paiute, but that did not matter. The Utah horses were hastily saddled, the skin bags were slung over the saddlehorns, and when Ki, who was not yet completely back in form, stumbled into camp, Jessie was saddling his horse.

"Get in the saddle!" she yelled as the samurai grabbed his bow and slung his quiver of arrows over his shoulder. "Now git!"

Medicine Joe grabbed the reins of the horse that Moses had been riding and bolted out into the lead. Ki was next, but Jessie, on the magnificent Appaloosa, quickly overtook them both.

"How many?" she yelled.

"Too many to fight! We've got to get Moses on our way out."

The howling Paiute swept after them, but their Indian ponies were thin and weak compared to the fine Utah horses. Ki, Jessie and Medicine Joe had no trouble lengthening the gap between themselves and their pursuers. The important thing, they all knew, was to pick Moses up, then pace their animals for the long days and nights ahead.

The Indians would realize that, while they might be outdistanced on the first hundred miles, they still had all the advantages. They alone knew the secret springs, the good water holes and the places where their horses could find grass enough to keep them going.

Jessie, like her companions, concentrated on making sure her horse did not step into a hole and break its leg. The Appaloosa wanted to surge through the brush and go around Medicine Joe, but Jessie kept the stallion in check.

She was about to ask exactly where they were going, when she heard the unmistakably loud explosion of Moses' huge buffalo rifle. Its heavy retort was instantly accompanied by the sound of a Winchester and then a six-gun as it banged rapidly.

Ki nocked an arrow on the run, and Medicine Joe had an old Army carbine gripped in his hands when they flew over the rise and saw that Moses had dropped his rifle and was bent over holding his stomach. One of the Paiute guards was down and not moving, but the other one was dragging himself forward with a six-gun clenched in his bloody fist.

Moses was helpless. The old mountain man was trying to pick up his rifle, but as he bent lower, his legs buckled and he fell to the ground. Medicine Joe let out a bloodcurdling scream and threw himself from his horse. He rolled and came up with his carbine aimed and firing at the crawling Paiute.

The Indian died kicking in the dirt. His pistol fell from his hand, and Medicine Joe raced to his old friend as Ki and Jessie caught up the man's stray horses.

When Medicine Joe reached his dying friend's side, he threw his head back and began to sing a death chant. Jessie dismounted, and one look at the mountain man's glazing eyes told her that the end was at hand for poor old Moses.

"You can't help him," she told the Shoshoni as a death rattle filled the mountain man's throat.

But Medicine Joe didn't seem to hear or care what Jessie said. He reloaded his carbine, still chanting, and when his friend shuddered and died, the death chant became even louder.

"Medicine Joe!" Ki said. "We *have* to ride away now. There are too many Paiute! They will kill us all no matter how bravely we fight."

The chant stilled in the Shoshoni's throat as he saw the first Paiute riders emerge on the horizon. Medicine Joe picked up his dead friend's buffalo rifle and reloaded it with calm resolve. "*You* ride, samurai. Take woman and go fast. I stay and fight." Ki judged the Paiute to be less than a mile away now. He was not afraid of death for himself, but his mission in life was to protect Jessie, and he couldn't help her in the desperate days that would come if he died in the next few minutes.

"If we live," Ki said, "someday we will visit your people and tell them of your bravery. You will become a legend among them. This I promise."

"I promise it too," Jessie said, as she remounted the Appaloosa.

Ki also mounted his horse, and they took the two extras, knowing that neither Moses nor Medicine Joe would ever need them again.

The last look Jessie had at the Shoshoni was one she would long remember. Medicine Joe's tobacco brown and deeply lined face were composed. The man resumed his death chant, as much for himself as for his white friend. The weariness slipped away from the Indian's face, and his expression was serene as he raised the big-bored rifle and took slow, deliberate aim. When the heavy buffalo rifle belched smoke and fire, it took a moment to see that the tall Paiute leader had disappeared from his racing horse. He had vanished as dramatically as if he'd been plucked up into the sky by the hand of God.

Ki waved a last farewell to Medicine Joe as the Shoshoni dropped the rifle and grabbed his own carbine. "Good hunting, my friend and thanks for saving my life."

"Yep," the old Shoshoni said as his rifle began to empty the saddles of even more Paiute ponies.

Ki and Jessie charged out of the Indian camp, and only
once did they dare to look back over their shoulders. It
was a mistake. They saw the Paiute clubbing the bodies of
Medicine Joe and Moses, and they heard the Shoshoni's
wails of fury and grief. It was a terrible sight, and Jessie
twisted back around in her saddle and concentrated her
attention on a set of low, sun-blasted hills due west,
toward Reno and the Sierra Nevada Mountains.

They slowed their horses to a ground-eating trot after
running them five hard miles. The Paiute were a good
mile behind them now, and they also slowed their ponies.

"It's going to come down to who can use their horses
the wisest," Jessie said.

"Let's change mounts."

They drew their horses to a standstill. Since Jessie was
leading the Shoshoni's Utah horse, she chose it to be her
second mount. The stirrups were too long, so she and Ki
used a few precious minutes to shorten them. When they
remounted, the Paiute were closing ground because their
ponies were still being ridden at a gallop.

"We'd better push it a little faster until we get some
more breathing room between us," Ki said.

Jessie agreed. Seeing about twenty Indian coming on
the run to have your scalp was pretty unnerving. She
was sure that the Indians were hoping that their quarry
would panic and run their horses to death, but she was
equally certain that that was not going to happen.

"Pace," she said, more for her own benefit than for
Ki's. "We can win if we just stay a couple of miles in
the lead. That's all we need."

Ki nodded in agreement. He had not once looked back

at the Paiute, but he knew exactly how close they were at any moment. "We will have to stop and rest sooner or later."

"We will when the Paiute are forced to stop." Jessie looked up at the sun, which was rapidly sinking. Night-time would be the best for travel, and she had little doubt that the Paiute would do everything in their power to catch them before dawn.

"We'll rest," she said, "but I don't think it will be until tomorrow. Tonight, we are going to break their spirits."

Even as she vowed to leave the Indians far behind, her lovely green eyes studied the ocean of brown, mostly treeless Nevada hills that rolled on and on, seemingly forever.

"It's going to come down to water," she said. "They know where it is, and we don't."

"But we have the skin bags filled," Ki reminded her. "Even though I realize that won't be enough water to take us to safety."

Jessie agreed. "That's why we are going to leave them so far behind before this night is over that they'll decide to give the chase up."

Ki said nothing. He had had many run-ins with the Apache and thought he knew them very well. Apache, once a member of their band had been killed, would never give up the chase until it became obvious that they would put themselves into a disastrous situation where they all might be killed.

But that was Apache. Neither Jessie nor he really knew much about Paiute. They might be stubborn or sensible. If they were stubborn, they'd take this chase all the way to Reno before being forced to abandon any chance for revenge.

Ki took a quick glance over his shoulder. The Paiute were still galloping, but they were fading back again. He sure hoped they were sensible Indians instead of stubborn.

Chapter 9

The desert crossing was two hundred miles of hell. One of the Utah horses broke a leg in a badger hole and had to be destroyed. Another animal suffered a stone bruise and was left behind. But the Appaloosa and the fourth horse carried Jessie and Ki on, and when they topped the Stillwater Range and plunged down into the Carson Sink, the Paiute went no farther.

"Look!" Jessie croaked with her throat parched and her lips chapped and bleeding. "Did you ever see such a beautiful sight?"

Ki managed a rare smile. "The United States Cavalry. No wonder the Paiute stopped coming."

Jessie and Ki pulled their horses to a shuddering standstill. Both animals were thin and worn down to the point of exhaustion. Frank Palmer's Appaloosa, however, looked as if it could run another few hundred miles.

Jessie and Ki dismounted. Jessie doffed her Stetson, and together they emptied the last of their precious water from their skin bags and gave it to the thirsty horses.

The cavalry patrol had spotted them and turned in their direction, moving at a brisk trot. But when they saw the Paiute warriors only a few miles behind, a bugle sounded and the soldiers broke into a gallop.

"Hold up!" the cavalry officer in command ordered when the patrol reached Jessie and Ki. "Company, halt!"

The officer was a six-footer with a salt-and-pepper mustache and the gold braid of a captain on his uniform. When he dismounted, a sergeant took his reins. The captain's eyes quickly appraised Jessie and Ki, especially noting the poor condition of their horses.

"I'd say you've ridden out of the valley of the damned," he said, watching the Paiute disappear.

"We've come from Salt Lake," Jessie wearily explained.

"And you made it without being scalped or dying of thirst? Quite remarkable! But why this way? Why didn't you follow the Humboldt River?"

"We thought it would be safer," Jessie confessed. "And that we might sneak through Paiute country without any fuss. Obviously, it did not work that way. Can you spare us some water?"

"Of course we can. Sergeant!"

The sergeant, a man in his late forties who looked like a tough barroom brawler but also a very competant soldier, in turn had one of the cavalrymen bring two canteens forward. Jessie and Ki drank greedily, and when they had satisfied their thirst, they wiped their mouths and expelled a sigh of relief.

"May I ask where you're going?" the captain said.

"To California," Jessie told him.

"I think it would be best if you accompanied me to nearby Fort Churchill, where we are doing our best to keep the Paiute under control."

Jessie nodded. "I hope it isn't far out of our way."

"Not at all. And from the looks of your horses, they could stand a little grain and hay."

"Yes," Jessie admitted. "I think that this has been very hard on these animals."

In a very few minutes, they were riding away, protected by the soldiers. Jessie and Ki both glanced back at the eastern hill, but the Paiute who had so doggedly chased them were nowhere to be seen.

The captain rode stirrup to stirrup beside Jessie, and he seemed eager to get acquainted. "May I ask why you and your friend were in such a hurry that you risked your lives to get here?"

"It concerns the Central Pacific Railroad," Jessie said, not wishing to elaborate.

"Oh," the captain said, "I understand they are having a very difficult time getting over Donner Pass."

"Really?"

"Yes, something about tunnel cave-ins. I don't know much about it. We have our hands full out here in the desert. Do you know anything about Fort Churchill?"

Jessie had a feeling she was going to hear all about it anyway, so she said, "Not a thing."

"It's the largest and most important military post in the Nevada Territory. It was built and staffed in 1860 after the Paiute burned out Williams Station and killed the Pony Express hostlers there. We've got more than six hundred soldiers now."

"Do you also protect the Central Pacific surveyors and bridge builders?"

"We do what we can, but it's hard," the captain said. "The Paiute fight like Apache—hit and run. They're too smart to engage us in any major skirmishes. They know they'd lose too many warriors."

Jessie nodded. She felt nothing but relief to finally be able to ride without constantly looking over her shoulder and pushing her horse to its limits.

The captain attempted to engage her further in conversation, but Jessie kept her answers short. After a while, the captain excused himself and rode out ahead of his column, leaving Jessie and Ki to the comfort of their own thoughts.

They remained two days at Fort Churchill, mainly for the sake of their horses. Ki's shoulder wound was inspected by the post surgeon, who pronounced it almost healed. His ribs were also mending nicely.

When they left the army outpost, Jessie could see the hazy blue outline of the Sierra Nevadas in the distance. They circled around Virginia City, which was booming with a gold and silver strike. Carson City was also crowded with miners and freight wagons, all feeding upon the Comstock Lode. But Jessie and Ki hardly bothered to ask about the fortunes of the Comstock. Instead, they rode straight north, passed around the west side of Washoe Lake, then arrived in Reno about sundown, to find a stable for their horses.

The Washoe Stable was owned by Mike McCormick, and it was located near the heart of the city, beside the Truckee River. Mike had once been a mustanger, but too many close calls with the Paiute had caused him to change his line of work.

He was in his late thirties, small but wiry, with a wife and seven children who were always either underfoot or about to get into some kind of mischief. But every stall in his barn was bedded with clean straw and had fresh water and plenty of good alfalfa hay brought over the Sierras from Sacramento by wagon.

"That Appaloosa is the best—and at the same time the worst—looking animal I've seen in a long time," Mike said, ignoring Ki's mount. "What happened to him?"

"Same thing that happened to my horse," Ki said. "We

had to outrun the Paiute for about three or four hundred miles."

Mike laughed. His tired-looking wife laughed too, holding their latest baby, and so did all his children. "Used to be I knew first-hand what you meant," Mike said. "Used to be, I was chasin' mustangs and Indians was chasin' me. Now, it's kids that are after me all the time."

Jessie laughed. "That sounds a lot more fun and quite a bit safer to me."

Mike stroked the Appaloosa's powerful neck. "You interested in selling this one?"

"Nope," Jessie said. "I borrowed him from a friend in Salt Lake City. The man expects to get him back."

"Too bad," the stable owner said.

"No it ain't," his wife said. "We ain't got no money to buy more horses."

Mike started to say something, but Jessie cut off an argument before it could get running. "Mike, I'd appreciate your feeding both these animals double rations until they're fat and sleek again."

"When will you be needing them?"

Jessie reached into her pockets and remembered she was broke. "I'll telegraph my banker in San Francisco tomorrow for cash. You'll be paid two months board in advance at the local bank, if that is all right with you."

"Why . . . why sure. But double rations will cost you extra."

"I know that. And I also want you to hire someone to curry them every day. Maybe one of your kids would like to earn an extra ten dollars."

The oldest, a boy of about nine, nodded his head vigorously.

"Good," Jessie said. "Now, if you'll tell us where the

best hotel in town is, we'll be on our way."

"That would be the Ponderosa, Miss Starbuck," Mike told her. "Just up the street on your left."

Jessie thanked the man and bid good evening to his family before she and Ki gathered their saddlebags and weapons and went straight to the hotel.

In the morning, Jessie spent her last few dollars on a big breakfast of buttered biscuits with honey, pork sausage, eggs and coffee. When she and Ki had had their fill, they went over to the telegraph office, and Jessie scribbled out a brief message to her San Francisco office, asking for five thousand dollars to be transferred to the Bank of Nevada immediately.

"Five thousand?" the telegraph operator asked, wanting to make sure that she had not made a mistake.

"Yes," Jessie said. "Immediately."

"Yes, ma'am."

Jessie watched as the message was sent over the wire. When it was acknowledged as received in San Francisco, she had to borrow two dollars from Ki to pay the operator.

"It will be ready by noon," she said to Ki with absolute confidence as they left the office and made their way back down Virginia Street.

Jessie thought Reno both quaint and picturesque. Now that the nearby Comstock Lode was generating millions of dollars worth of ore and the Central Pacific Railroad was due to come through town, real estate and commerce were booming. New buildings were in construction everywhere, and yet, Reno had a sure confidence about itself that said it would not be just another boom town destined to go bust.

"If I had more time," Jessie said, "I would buy some

72

property here, if for no other reason than pure speculation. This town has the feel of another Denver to me."

"What about Central Pacific Railroad stocks? Do you
really intend to buy them?"

"Yes," Jessie said decisively. "If we are going to go
up to the summit tunnels with the idea of risking our lives
to make it a success, it seems to me only reasonable that
I should also be willing to invest in the project. Don't
you agree?"

"Why not?" Ki said.

Later that evening, Jessie read a copy of the *Reno
Gazette* and learned that, indeed, the Central Pacific
Railroad was having more than its share of construction
problems. Apparently, some of the Irish were angry at
being replaced by Chinese and had been harassing the
Celestials and causing a good deal of trouble for the
railroad.

Charles Crocker and Harvey Strobridge were reported as saying that they would not tolerate hooliganism.
They'd rehire the displaced Irishmen only if they were
willing to behave and work hard. They'd even make sure
that no Irishman faced the humiliation of having to take
orders from a Chinaman. But by God, they both said,
the more than four thousand Chinese currently on their
payroll were staying and that was that!

"When the two railroads finally get to moving across
the desert, I expect many of those who work on the transcontinental will remain out west. Quite a few might even
stay in Reno," Jessie said.

Ki agreed. "And I think many of them will be coming to work the Comstock Lode. I overheard men on the
street crowing about how the Comstock promises to be
an even bigger strike than the Forty-Niner Gold Rush."

"That is hard to believe," Jessie said. "Usually, those

73

things peter out about as fast as they blossom. But the Comstock is deep mining, and no one can say how much ore is still buried under Virginia City."

At noon, they went to the bank, and Jessie's money was ready on account. The bank manager, a Mr. J. L. Bolton, was all smiles. "Why, Miss Starbuck of Texas, what an honor to serve you! I've read about you for years, and your fame just keeps spreading. You're going to be as well remembered as your late father, God rest his soul."

Jessie took the banker's proffered hand and shook it firmly. "Thank you, Mr. Bolton. But I began life with a head start. By the time I was old enough to realize who I was, my father was already rich and famous. All I've tried to do is to build on his accomplishments."

"And you have! Oh, you most certainly have," the banker said.

Jessie thanked the man for his compliments. She was always a little uncomfortable when praised, but that, too, was something that came from being her father's only child. Alex Starbuck had never liked praise, only results. He'd started out as an importer and exporter of goods in a small office in San Francisco and grown to be one of the most prosperous men in the world. Shipping, banking, transportation, ranching and mining were the fields where he'd amassed his fortune.

"I need transportation to the Central Pacific Railroad construction site," Jessie said. "Where would I find it in this town?"

The banker looked surprised but quickly recovered. "Well, I'd say that Dan Decker's small but reliable stageline would deliver you up there reasonably fast."

"And where would I find Mr. Decker?"

The banker gave her directions, and as Jessie was

leaving, he said, "Excuse me for asking, but have you become a large holder of Central Pacific Railroad stock?"

"No," Jessie said. "Not yet at least. But I expect that will change once I have had a first-hand look at the railroad's progress."

"I see. I see." The banker seemed very interested in this. "Well," he said, clearing his throat with self-importance. "I must tell you that the railroad seems to be having great difficulty in the Sierras. However, as I'm sure you must know, the government has granted them alternating twenty–square-mile sections of free land in addition to very generous cash of forty-eight thousand for every mile of track laid."

"Yes," Jessie said, "I know. But everything that the Central Pacific uses, every rail, every locomotive and every railroad car, has to be shipped all the way around Cape Horn. That is very, very expensive indeed. And no one is quite sure yet how a train can pull the grades that will be asked of it going over those high mountains."

"Are you saying the project is doomed from the very start?" the banker asked.

"Of course not. I'm just saying that it will be very, very difficult. I am quite sure the transcontinental railroad will be completed before the end of this decade."

The banker's eyebrows rose with surprise. "How encouraging to hear someone like yourself give the railroad such a vote of absolute confidence! I think I might buy some stock in the effort now that I've had the benefit of your wisdom."

"Do that," Jessie said. "But don't invest your depositors' funds."

She winked, and the banker finally caught on to the fact that he was being teased. He chuckled, and his assistant, a Mr. Nichols, chuckled as well.

Jessie and the samurai left to find Dan Decker. The day was still young, and the Sierras stood out boldly against the western sky as if daring Jessie to come and sample their cold, clean air.

After the ordeal she and Ki had just gone through in crossing the great deserts of Utah and Nevada, Jessie welcomed the cool mountain air and the scent of pines.

Yes, she thought, and no more blood-lusting Paiute Indians, either. All that she would have to face now was the infamous Donner Pass.

Chapter 10

Dan Decker was a heavyset man, grimy, unwashed and smelly. He had a terrible cowlick, and his nose had been fist-broken so many times that it resembled mashed peaches. When he smiled—which was not often—his front gold teeth drew your attention, and when he growled it came all the way up from his bulging belly. Decker's arms, chest and shoulders were the thickest Jessie had ever seen. He looked and was immensely strong.

"Now why," he demanded, "would a lady like yourself want to go up and spend time at Donner Pass with the rabble?"

"I'd like to see the railroad being constructed."

"It's not going anywhere soon," Decker said. "They're blocked at Donner Summit, and soon they'll be buried up to their smokestacks in snow."

"All the more reason I should get up there while the weather is still holding," Jessie said. "There is a touch of autumn in the air."

"It'll be freezing already at night up there," the freighter snapped. "Is your Chinaman friend looking for work as one of Crocker's Pets? That's what they're being called by us, you know."

"I'm not Chinese," Ki interrupted stiffly. "I'm samurai. Half-white and half-Japanese."

Decker turned to Ki. They were about the same height, but the ox-shouldered freighter was at least seventy pounds heavier. "Is that a fact? And what the hell is a samurai?"

"He's a warrior," Ki said, sensing that Decker was a very aggressive man who loved to exhibit his strength. Ki did not judge the man to be vicious, only vain when it came to his physical dominence of other men.

"A warrior? You mean like a damned Injun?"

"No," Ki said patiently. "A samurai warrior has learned the art of *te*. It's our word for open-hand fighting, in which a man's body becomes his best weapon."

"I can understand that." Decker raised his clenched right fist. "You see those knuckles? They're *my* best weapon. I've got a broken nose, sure. But it looked like this before I was sixteen, a boy fighting men. Ever since, I been payin' men back. Breakin' *their* noses and faces."

"I see," Ki said. "The difference between us is that I seek to hurt no one. I fight only when given no choice, or to protect Miss Starbuck. I do not like to hurt other men." Ki shrugged. "Sometimes, my enemies give me no choice but to fight."

"You don't look strong enough to worry anyone," the freighter said out of the side of his mouth. He hooked his thumbs into his baggy pants and said to Jessie, "Does this little fella think he's going to protect you against the kind of men you'll run into out in the West?"

Jessie did not appreciate the way this brute was trying

to make Ki look weak and cowardly. He was attempting to pick a fight, but Jessie was not going to allow it, not with Ki still on the mend.

"Mr. Decker, what my friend is or isn't is none of your business. I want to pay you to take us both to Donner Summit. If you would rather fight than work, then we will find another freighter. Now, are you a businessman or a brawler?"

Decker smiled. "I've got my bills to pay, same as we all do," he said. "It's just that I never saw a warrior in action before. And being a man that likes to test his own mettle, I thought—"

"I don't care what you thought," Jessie said, cutting the man off in midsentence. "Ki, I think we have heard enough of this bully. Let's find someone else."

"No! No, wait," Decker said, all the bluster washing out of him. "I'd like your business, and I'll deliver you at Donner Summit for a fair price."

"How soon?"

"We can leave first thing tomorrow morning," Decker said. "I'll have a buggy ready, and we'll be at the construction camp by tomorrow evening."

Jessie looked at Ki, who nodded that it was fine with him. "All right," Jessie said. "Tomorrow morning at first light."

Decker, realizing that he had almost lost a good commission, sighed with relief. "Good," he said, sticking out his hand, which Jessie took, and then saying, "I meant no offense, ma'am."

"None taken," Jessie said.

"None to you either, samurai," Decker growled, extending his hand to Ki.

Ki knew the freighter would crush his hand in a grip

like a bear trap. The samurai's hands were his weapons, and he was not about to enter this trap, so he left his hand at his side.

Decker made a big point of looking down at Ki's hand and then his own. His round cheeks flamed with humiliation, and then he turned and stomped away.

"What's the matter with him?" Jessie asked.

"It's simple enough," Ki said. "He wanted to impress you at my expense."

Jessie wasn't pleased. "If we had time, I'd look around for a better man."

"He'll do all right," Ki said. "He's like a horse that's been allowed to get away with a few bad habits. He just needs to be taught some humility and respect."

"He needs to have his nose reshaped once or twice more," Jessie said.

Ki agreed. And he knew that he had angered and shamed Decker by refusing to allow the bigger man to crush his hand in a childish show of his superior strength.

The samurai knew he was in for a fight. But with his shoulder and ribs still mending, it would have to be a very quick fight, or he would find himself on the losing end.

The next morning, they left Reno at daybreak, and Decker drove in silence out of town, climbing the gentle slope of the Sierra foothills and passing many big freight wagons that were hauling timbers down from the higher elevations.

"Why so much logging?" Jessie asked. "Surely Reno isn't growing that fast."

"Hell no it isn't," Decker said. "Most all the timber you see is going to the big sawmills just east of town.

80

They saw then haul it up to Virginia City, Gold Hill and Silver City. Them Comstock mines swallow up thousands of board feet every week."

"I see," Jessie said. "Yes, I'm sure that they do, with their deep mining."

Decker shook his head. "Some folks say that those Comstock mines will eat up a hundred miles of this eastern Sierra slope before the gold and silver peter out."

"I hope not."

"Don't matter one way or the other to me," Decker said. "It's money that makes things work. People with jobs and business spendin' their money. Them without don't spend anything. Money puts food on my table and whiskey in my glass."

Jessie said nothing. She could see places where the mountainsides had been stripped of trees, some of which had been several hundred years old. She guessed that, if this kind of devastation did not abate, there would be mud slides and floods plaguing Reno in the years to come.

The Truckee River was quite low at this time of year, and they had no trouble fording it several times as they followed its general course up to the summit.

"This is the same route the railroad will use when it lays its tracks," Decker said. "I personally don't think they will ever get over the summit, but if they do, it will be one hell of a job just coming down this canyon."

Jessie agreed that the canyon was steep and seemed a very unlikely route for a train. But with trestles daring engineers, she supposed that a railroad bed could be constructed.

The last five miles were the steepest, and the team of horses really had their work cut out for them as Decker whipped and worried them up toward the rocky summit. Off to their left and right Jessie saw deep-blue alpine lakes fed by snow. The air was thin and cool at this altitude; the sky overhead was cobalt blue and cloudless. At last they crested the mountaintop to see thousands of Chinese working feverishly down below.

Decker pulled his out-of-breath team to a standstill and pointed down through the timber to his left. "Over there is where the Donner Party got trapped and ate each other."

Jessie did not appreciate the man's choice of words but decided not to comment. Instead, she studied the place where, in the terrible winter of 1846, forty-five members of the ill-fated Donner Party had perished after suffering months of winter blizzards and starvation.

"Up there on the trees, some forty feet above the ground, you can see where the Donner Party made ax marks," Decker said. "In the middle of winter, the snow will get that deep."

"Is that why they are tunneling under the summit?" Jessie asked.

"Yep," the freighter said. "Them tunnels have got to be blasted out of solid rock. I heard that Crocker and Strobridge have been having a hell of a time making progress. That black powder just won't do the job. There is talk about using nitroglycerine, but I don't know about that. I hear it's mighty dangerous stuff."

Jessie had heard the same thing. In fact, several years earlier a chemist who'd been experimenting with the highly unstable explosive had leveled an entire San Francisco city block, and the city had quickly yielded to public outrage and outlawed the liquid explosive.

Decker's winded horses finally caught their breath, and the man drove them down a steep, winding road toward the vast armylike construction camp.

Jessie's first impression was that this Central Pacific construction camp was very different from the Union Pacific camp, which was now laying rails across Wyoming. One major reason was that where the Irish had preferred to live in their high, three-tiered railroad sleeping coaches, the Chinese liked to make their own camps and congregate off by themselves.

Jessie also knew that the Chinese insisted on buying and cooking their own food. This represented a great savings for the Central Pacific and neither Crocker nor his business partners had objected to the practice, even though the Chinese also insisted on a short morning and afternoon tea break.

When Decker's buggy approached the edge of the bustling camp, Jessie said, "I believe we can find either Mr. Crocker or Mr. Strobridge on our own. Here is your money."

Decker reined in his horses and made a big show of counting his wages. "There's only fifty dollars here."

"That's what we agreed upon."

"I want another twenty. It's only fair because you said you wanted to reach Donner Summit. I brought you farther by coming the extra way down to this camp. It's another four or five miles at least."

Jessie and Ki dismounted from the buggy, and Jessie tried to keep her temper under control.

"Mr. Decker, I assumed that you understood that we wanted to be delivered to this camp. Any reasonable person would make that assumption. No, I will not pay you an additional twenty dollars."

Decker hopped to the ground and began to shake his buggy whip. "I think you'd better pay me," he yelled. "I'm only askin' what I got coming!"

Ki stepped between them, and when the man drew back his lash and sent it whistling toward the samurai's

83

face, Ki ducked, took a half-step forward and then sent a foot-strike to Decker's midsection that drove the brute back two steps and caused his breath to explode outward.

"Why you slant-eyed son of a bitch!" Decker roared. He lashed out again, only to see the samurai throw an arm up to catch the whip.

Decker yanked hard and pulled Ki off his feet. Instead of finding his opponent off-balance, Decker grunted with pain as Ki delivered a hard knife-hand blow to the base of his neck.

A normal man would have dropped like a stone. But Decker was horse-strong, and he merely staggered before charging into Ki's sweep lotus that caught him under the chin and lifted him off the ground.

Decker landed in a heap. He shook his head, crawled to his feet and came in windmilling with his fists. You could say one thing in his favor: he was not a quitter.

Ki took one blow, and it made the entire right side of his face go numb. He staggered and set his feet, and when Decker lunged at him with outstretched arms, Ki unleashed a wicked snap-kick to Decker's groin that made his face drain of color. Decker grabbed his crotch and collapsed in a writhing pile.

"A man like you don't need a gun, does he?" a deep voice said from behind them.

Both Ki and Jessie turned around to face a man who could be none other than Harvey Strobridge, the Central Pacific's chief of construction. Nobody could mistake the black patch over Strobridge's eye and his air of authority.

"Mr. Strobridge," Jessie said, noticing how the Chinese workers had stopped for a moment to see Ki in action and how they were trying to suppress smiles, "I am pleased to make your acquaintance."

84

Strobridge was all business and definitely not the kind of man who fawned over a beautiful woman. He nodded curtly and said, "I don't know who that big son of a bitch is that your friend just dismantled, but we haven't time for fighting here. And this is no tourist attraction, so you'll have to be on your way."

"I think I had better explain," Jessie said. "But we need to do so in private."

Strobridge scowled. He was big and raw-boned, rugged-looking and impatient. "Explain what?"

Jessie moved close to the man. "Explain the fact that your railroad, like the Union Pacific that we left two weeks ago, is under siege and being sabotaged."

Strobridge's eyes widened. "What the. . . . "

"Not here," Jessie said. "I will only speak to you or to Mr. Crocker, and then in private."

Strobridge frowned, scratched his head and studied Jessie very closely. "Lady," he said at long last. "You sure have got me confused. Why don't you and your dangerous friend just hang around for about an hour until we knock off for the day? After that, I'll take you to meet Mr. Crocker, and we can sit down and see what you are all about."

"That's an excellent suggestion," Jessie said.

"What about him?" Strobridge asked, pointing to Decker, who was still cradling his testicles.

"Oh," Ki said, "I think he'll go back to Reno without raising any more trouble."

Strobridge allowed himself the thinnest of smiles. "If I'd taken a kick in the balls like he did, I wouldn't trust myself to even move for about a week."

"He gave me no choice," Ki explained. "He'd been looking for trouble all the way up here. I think he just likes to fight."

85

"That might change after today," Strobridge opined. "Now if you'll excuse me, I've got a tunnel to bore, and it isn't going too damn well."

"Are you using nitroglycerine yet?"

Strobridge had started to turn and walk away, but Jessie's question stopped him in his tracks. "Now whatever gave you such an idea?"

Jessie shrugged. First impressions were often the truest impressions, and Strobridge seemed to be a hard, blunt but fair and honest man. She decided that she would be honest and direct with him.

"If you aren't using it," she said, "you ought to be."

"You an engineer or chemist?"

"No," Jessie said. "But I can bring either one up here and they'll tell you the same thing."

"Lady," Strobridge said, "I'm going to look forward to sitting down with Crocker and your friend and having a conversation. There's more to you than good looks."

"Damn right there is," Jessie said with a smile. "And I'm glad that you can see that right away, so we can dispense with the usual condescending treatment a woman receives from a rugged construction man like yourself."

Strobridge liked that. He even barked a rusty laugh before he strode away, yelling and giving orders to the swarming Chinese workmen.

"You impressed him," Ki said.

"So did you," Jessie replied. "Do you think we had better get Decker up into his buggy and help him get headed back to Reno?"

Ki nodded. He and Jessie managed to help the powerful man to his feet and guide him to his buggy. When Decker was in his seat and still very pale, Ki handed the man his lines and said, "I saw a snowpack up there on

86

the summit less than a few hundred yards from the road we came over."

"So?" Decker wheezed.

"So sit on it awhile and your testicles won't swell up to the size of apples."

Decker studied him with slightly glazed eyes. "If I ever see you in Reno, I'll take you apart next time. You just got lucky with those damn feet. But two can play the same dirty game. A real man fights with his fists."

"I'll try to remember that the next time I'm attacked," Ki facetiously promised as he stepped back and watched the suffering bully drive away.

Chapter 11

Jessie had heard a great deal about Charles Crocker and knew what to expect. He was said to be a huge man, weighing in at somewhere between 250 and 300 pounds. According to almost everyone, Crocker was brutish, profane and foul-tempered. Raised by a saloon keeper in Troy, New York, Crocker had journeyed west to become a hard-working, hard-drinking blacksmith. Eventually he wound up in California and quickly realized there was more profit to be made in selling goods to the argonauts than in panning gold.

In only a few years, Crocker, despite his irascible nature, became a wealthy dry-goods merchant. Now, as the man ultimately in charge of construction operations, his enormous drive and energy were exactly the qualities that were needed to push the Central Pacific over the Sierras.

Crocker and Strobridge were quite a pair. Both stood well over six feet and Crocker was smoking a cigar. When he saw Jessie he blinked with surprise, but he did not smile or give any indication that he was pleased to see her.

"Crocker here," he said, ignoring Ki and towering over

Jessie. "Harvey tells me you used the word 'sabotage' a while ago. Is that correct?"

It would have been easy for Jessie to be intimidated by the big man and his lack of civility, but she stood her ground and tried not to allow his damned smelly cigar to make her nauseous.

"That's right," she said. "My name is Jessica Starbuck and this is my friend Ki."

"Jessica Starbuck of Starbuck Enterprises?"

"That's right."

Crocker looked at her with even more interest. "I never had the pleasure of making your father's acquaintance. He died before I even arrived in California. But I've heard about him for years. He was supposed to have been brilliant, resourceful and lucky."

"He never believed in luck," Jessie said. "He believed that those who trust in luck always end up losers."

Crocker barked a deep laugh. "Is that a fact! Did he never play games of chance? Poker? Faro? Roulette?"

"No," Jessie said. "He was not a gambler, though many who watched him amass his fortune said he often took risks. But he told me that, in business, unlike games of chance, a smart man at least knows the odds."

Crocker wore a look of amusement. He glanced at his superintendant, the stern, one-eyed Harvey Strobridge, and said, "Harvey, what do you think of that kind of reasoning?"

"I don't believe in luck either," Strobridge said. "I believe in hard work."

"Yes," Crocker said, "and so do I."

He sighed and gazed up toward Donner Summit. "But I'm not sure that even hard work will get us to Nevada at the rate we are going and with winter coming on so soon in these high mountains."

For a moment, they all read his dark thoughts, and then Crocker swung his eyes on Ki. "You ain't no Chinaman, are you? What, half-white and. . . . "

"Half-Japanese," Ki said. "I was trained a samurai."

Crocker's eyebrows rose and he actually smiled. "Is that a fact! It might surprise you, but I know a thing or two about the Orient, its people and its customs. You see, it was my idea to try the Chinese when our Irish went on strike. Isn't that right, Harvey?"

Strobridge nodded stiffly, and Jessie remembered that the tall New England engineer had been quite opposed to the idea, but Crocker had insisted, and the Chinese had quickly proven their worth.

"Yes," Crocker continued, "the Chinese are our salvation. We have scoured San Francisco for them, and now five thousand of them work here, and I have a man in Canton recruiting even more. I'll take all that I can get at two dollars a day, and they are worth twice that if we can best these accursed Sierras."

Jessie watched the Chinese as a new shift filed past on their way up the mountainside to work on Summit Tunnel. They were quite small, no longer than her, and most did not weigh much if anything over one hundred pounds. They were all dressed the same, in the blue cotton denim of the Orient, and wore huge basket hats that looked very much like umbrellas.

As they passed, they looked furtively up at Crocker and Strobridge and smiled, then dropped their eyes and shuffled quickly by.

"They call me 'Cholly Clocker' and Harvey, 'Boss Man.' They respect us, though, and I like to pay them every month with my own hand in gold coin. They're loyal and willing. I don't dare to tell you how many of them have already died working up here and how many more will die before we break through the tunnel and finally reach the Nevada deserts."

"And there is nothing that can be done to prevent it?" Ki asked.

"Sure," Strobridge said. "We could shut down for the winter and let the Union Pacific gobble up the easy land and money incentives. Then this railroad would go broke, and it might be another ten or twenty years until anyone was willing to try and push it over the summit. It would just stop here."

"That would be very unfortunate," Jessie said. "No one wants that to happen."

Crocker's expression darkened. "Then we have no choice but to beat at this mountain until it is defeated, and many of the Chinese will die this winter."

Jessie knew that Crocker was right. He had a stubborn, jutting jaw, and everything about both him and Strobridge gave the impression of men who would die trying before becoming quitters.

Crocker had rapidly smoked his cigar down to a smelly nubbin. He tossed it to the earth, ground it into extinction with his heel, then said to Jessie, "What's this sabotage business you mentioned?"

In as few words as possible, Jessie told the two Central Pacific men about the recent sabotage that had plagued the Union Pacific as it moved across Wyoming. Crocker and Strobridge listened with great interest, and when Jessie was finished, they were both grim and tight-lipped.

"I tell you," Strobridge said with a sad shake of his head, "we have had more than our share of accidents. Seems like they happen about once a week, and when they do, the poor Chinese are always the victims."

Crocker was more specific. "Like the Union Pacific,

we also push flatcars ahead of our locomotives as we lay track. The flatcars transport our supply of railroad ties, tons of rails, kegs of black powder and spikes, and even the lumber needed to build our trestles. They tote everything we need to lay the track. Well, last week another one broke loose."

"Then it's happened before?" Jessie asked.

"Damn right it has!" Strobridge blurted in exasperation. "And this last time it sent four flatcars loaded with tools, iron rails and track rushing right off the end of a trestle bridge. Killed five good Chinamen, and it cost us three days of lost time. Messed up the trestle we just spent two weeks constructing and made a hell of a mess down in the gorge. Even the rails that went over the edge were so twisted we couldn't use them. It was a great expense in time and materials. We still haven't completed the trestle repairs. But the Chinese never backed down from the risks. They just keep working. Sunup to sundown with almost no rest except for their short tea breaks. They aren't afraid of anything."

Crocker nodded energetically and said to Jessie, "That's the truth. Have you ever heard of the Cape Horn of the Sierras?"

"No."

"Well," Crocker said, "it's a mountain of pure granite that is harder than diamonds. It rises about a thousand feet over the treacherous American River, and it blocked our path. There wasn't even a handhold on its rock face, and yet, our surveyors told us there was no way to lay track around it."

Crocker paused, selected another cigar and bit the end off of it. He knew that he had Jessie and Ki's full attention, and he obviously enjoyed creating a moment of suspense in his story. "Tell 'em what happened, Harvey." he said, lighting his cigar and inhaling deeply.

Strobridge was happy to finish the story, but he was not Crocker's equal in dramatizing an account. "Well," he said, "the Chinese found a way to build a railroad bed up the side of that rock face."

"How?" Ki asked.

"They lowered themselves down from the top in reed baskets, and they chiseled bore holes into the face of Cape Horn. They poured black powder into those holes and blasted out a ledge, inch by bloody inch."

"A ledge?" Jessie asked.

"That's right," Crocker said. "Wasn't nothing more than that for months. I used to watch them dangle at the end of long ropes in those flimsy baskets and feel my own heart pound faster. Now and then, a basket would tear apart and drop a couple of them to their deaths, but that never stopped more from going down the side. Month after month, the Chinese widened it, until finally we had a roadbed that climbed the face of that cliff. I'll tell you, whenever a train climbs Cape Horn, everybody on board holds their breath, but it's safe."

Jessie and Ki were deeply impressed. Jessie said, "If you can beat something like Cape Horn, I'd think that Donner Summit wouldn't worry you too much."

Crocker exhaled a stream of blue, noxious smoke but was thoughtful enough to do it in someplace other than Jessie's face. "Miss Starbuck, it's not a matter of *if* we'll conquer the summit, but *when*. And given the Union Pacific's much faster progress, if we don't push through the last tunnel this winter and get down this mountain by spring to race east, we're going to go broke and our individual investors will desert us like fleas off a dyin' dog."

93

"It's that bad?"

"Damn right!" Crocker swore. "The Union Pacific, at last I heard, has pushed their line almost three hundred miles westward. We're still less than a hundred miles east of Sacramento, where we started!"

Jessie understood. Everyone from President Lincoln on down had felt from the beginning that the Sierras were by far the most formidable obstacle to be overcome by either railroad.

Strobridge added, "Last winter, snow drifted across the roadbed sometimes forty feet deep, and we had men buried alive by avalanches. Can you imagine working between two narrow walls of snow and ice forty feet high? The Chinese froze, lost fingers and toes. It was so bad that we ceased construction for three months and took care of the Chinese in Sacramento until the snow began to melt up here. This winter will be even worse because we're higher."

Crocker studied the tip of his ash and said in a surprisingly quiet voice, "Miss Starbuck, despite the losses we suffered last winter, this winter we have no choice but to push on and try to be in Reno by spring. If we aren't, we'll go belly up because all the real profit is going to be made by driving the rails across the deserts of Utah and Nevada."

"And I'm afraid even that won't be too easy," Jessie cautioned. "We just came across those deserts and lost two good men to the Paiute."

Crocker knitted his brows. "After what we've been facing up in these damned Sierras, there is nothing that the Indians can do to scare me or my workmen. So far, we've drilled and beat our way through fourteen tunnels, most of them over a thousand feet long, and nobody thought we'd make it past Dutch Flat. Now, we've got just one more tunnel to go, but it's the worst by far because it's the hardest rock in the world. Some days, we don't make an honest foot of headway and that with three shifts of Chinese working around the clock."

"I mentioned nitroglycerine," Jessie said, "Have you tried it?"

"No," Crocker answered. "But we may have to. You see, in the tunnels, black powder leaves so much smoke that you can't go back to work for almost an hour after each blast. And sometimes, all the powder just blows out the hole and hardly breaks the new rock. Black powder just isn't much use on this granite."

"I can help you find a chemist," Jessie said. "I know that it's dangerous, but if black powder isn't working, I see no other way to push on through."

Crocker studied her closely. "Let's get back to the issue of sabotage. Who and why?"

"We uncovered a ring of saboteurs on the Union Pacific west of Cheyenne," Jessie explained. "I believe they have a large financial stake in getting Congress— or you—to abandon this project so that this country's first transcontinental railroad can be rerouted across the south."

Crocker was not a man easily shocked, but now he was. "Miss Starbuck!" he exclaimed. "I have no reason to doubt you are sincere, but certainly your fears are ungrounded."

"No," Ki said, "they are not. West of Cheyenne your rivals were also having a terrible time because of a rash of accidents that were costly in respect to both lives and property. Miss Starbuck and I were asked by our friend, Mr. Hugh Hollister, to investigate and assist. We did that and eventually uncovered the local ringleader, who was killed. Unfortunately, we were unable to find out who was really behind the plot."

Crocker and Strobridge studied each other for a long moment, and then Crocker said, "I know Mr. Hollister and also the chief of construction, Butler Benton. I would insist on communicating with them by telegraph to verify your stories."

"By all means, do that," Jessie said. "Mr. Hollister was poisoned but is recovering nicely in Cheyenne. I am sure that both he and Mr. Benton will confirm everything we have just revealed."

"Good," Strobridge said. "We will have our reply by tomorrow, and if what you say is confirmed, then we have to admit we have underestimated the extent of our problems. Up to now, all we have been doing is trying to beat these mountains. We never dreamed that we were also pitted against some kind of diabolical conspiracy."

"I know," Jessie said. "As if these mountains were not enough of a challenge."

Crocker sighed. "We *will* overcome every obstacle," he vowed. "My partners are doing their jobs, and we will do ours to see this thing through. Tomorrow, I'll take you into the summit tunnel and show you how we are attacking the brute."

"We don't want to be a bother," Jessie said. "And we know that you've got a job to do here. Perhaps if we could. . . . "

"No, no!" Crocker insisted. "I'd be inspecting all four faces of the tunnel we are working anyway."

"Four?"

"Yes," Crocker said, "you couldn't see the work from the Truckee Canyon supply road that comes up from Reno, but we are also tunneling in from the eastern slope of the summit."

"Good idea," Jessie said. "That way the work will go twice as fast. But that's only two faces."

"Wrong," Crocker said. "It was Mr. Strobridge's brilliant idea that we sink a shaft right in the center of the tunnel and then start working it in both directions."

Jessie and Ki were amazed. Crocker and Strobridge were ingenious! This way, there would be four gangs of Chinese tunneling simultaneously. And if what Crocker said was true, about the summit granite being so hard that some days only a foot of progress could be made, then even with four gangs drilling and blasting, it would still take a long time to tunnel under the Donner Summit.

"How long is the summit tunnel going to be?" Ki asked.

"A quarter of a mile," Strobridge said, "give or take ten feet."

Jessie did a very quick calculation in her head. Knowing how many feet there were in a mile, she judged a quarter of a mile would still be well over thirteen hundred feet. Going through solid rock, that was quite a task.

Chapter 12

They had been given berths in a fine railroad coach. Early the next morning, Jessie and Ki watched Charles Crocker put away an enormous breakfast of Belgian waffles smothered under fresh strawberries, bacon, venison and eggs, with apple tarts for dessert.

When the rotund Crocker was finished eating, he pushed himself ponderously to his feet, smacked his lips and said, "This high mountain air gives a body a hell of an appetite. I never felt better."

"Your meals here are excellent," Jessie said.

"You're damn right they are," Crocker said. "I told my partners that I'd boss the construction, and they could live in the refinement of the big cities—but I'd do it only on the condition that I ate and slept well. My coach is a rolling palace. The chef I chose is a genius, and at the end of a hard day, I enjoy my luxuries. Now, shall we go see the tunnel?"

Jessie and Ki nodded and then followed the railroad man out into the chill air. The sky overhead was leaden, and there was a stiff wind blowing from the west. Crocker buttoned up his coat and jammed a cigar into his mouth. "I'm afraid the first snow is going to fall before much longer."

"But it's still only October," Jessie said.

Crocker turned his back to the wind and struggled with several matches before he finally managed to light his cigar. When he pivoted around to face Jessie and Ki, he said, " 'Only October,' you say? My dear young woman, the Donner Party was trapped at the end of October with the year's first winter blizzard. And for your further information, October blizzards are not uncommon at this elevation."

"I see," Jessie said, standing corrected. "So what do you do when the snows fall? Surely the Chinese can't survive in those flimsy canvas tents."

"They can and they *must* survive," Crocker said. "Any day now, we should be receiving thousands of heavy woolen coats, gloves and trousers that have been ordered since early last spring. For warmth, I'll double the ax crews so that just as many men are chopping firewood as railroad ties. The desperate work of tunneling never stops, but we'll have to stop road grading during the blizzards."

Crocker puffed rapidly on his cigar, and the wind made sparks fly from the cherry-red tip. "The wind is the worst part of it," he said. "It howls over this pass and drives icicles into a man's bones. But wind or no wind and no matter how cold and deep the snow, the Chinese will work out in the open. They understand the terms of this railroad—no work, no pay. Besides, they'll keep warmer on the job than sitting around a campfire."

Both Ki and Jessie could imagine what a bitterly cold experience working here would be in a few months. Even now, Jessie was shivering in the wind as they waited impatiently until a buckboard loaded with kegs of black powder came bouncing up to join them.

"This is our ride up to the summit," Crocker explained, offering Jessie his big paw and helping her into the seat. "Ki, I didn't think you'd mind sitting in back."

Ki studied the kegs of black powder without anxiety. Unlike nitroglycerine, black powder was very stable and would not explode unless it came in contact with a spark. But with the wind blowing and Crocker smoking in the buckboard seat, a spark might well be whipped back and settle on a keg.

Ki had no wish to challenge the overbearing railroad tycoon, but he knew he had to make an issue of the cigar. "Mr. Crocker, I don't mind in the least riding in the back of this wagon, but I would appreciate it if you'd extinguish that cigar."

Crocker's bushy eyebrows raised in question. "Ahh! Nothing to worry about."

But the samurai stood rooted beside the wagon. "It is not for my own safety that I ask this favor, but for Jessie's."

Crocker wasn't pleased, but he tossed the cigar out anyway, and Ki extinguished it with his heel before he climbed onto the wagonbed.

The driver was a small, taciturn Irishman, and as he drove up toward the summit, Jessie saw that most of the foremen and many of the tracklayers were Irish. This was in contrast to the road-grading crews, who were exclusively Chinese. The Chinese reminded Ki of swarming ants the way they attacked the roadbed with their picks, shovels and little handcarts. They were in perpetual motion. Not hurried or erratic, but steady and unceasing in their effort to level a roadbed for the oncoming tracklayers.

As on the Union Pacific racing westward across Wyoming, the tracklayers were fed rails off the first flatcar, five men to each five-hundred-pound length of iron. The tracklayers grunted and sweated even in the cold air, and their muscles bulged with exertion.

Farther on, Ki and Jessie saw that the axmen and drillers were mostly Chinese, but the Irish were in charge of setting off the explosives.

Jessie said, "I notice that the Irish and Chinese seem to work well together. Has this always been the case?"

"Hell no!" Crocker snapped. "At first, they hated the Chinese with a passion, but after watching them at Cape Horn, they changed their minds. Now, Irish, Chinese and my Mexicans get along fine. The problem is, I can't keep anyone but Chinese on the payroll. The others work here just long enough to get a stake, then they head off to the gold fields convinced that they'll soon strike it rich. Most of 'em return in a few weeks with their tails between their legs, broke, hungry, needing a job again."

"And you rehire them?"

"Sure," Crocker said. "I'm so short of laborers that I'll take a man even if he'll only give me a few honest days of work. And the truth be known, my wages can't compete with what they're paying on the Comstock. But then, I'd think this was a lot better work than being down in some deep mine where it's hellish hot and you're wondering if the roof is going to drop on your head and bury you alive."

"I agree," Jessie said. "But some men can't think beyond the end of the week's paycheck."

They rode in silence the rest of the way up to the summit. The scenery was spectacular, and despite the cold bite of the wind, Jessie was glad that she and Ki had been invited to accompany Crocker up to the summit to see how the work was progressing on the great summit tunnel.

The driver pulled the team to a halt in the lee of a some rocks while Jessie, Crocker and Ki climbed down. Chinese appeared to unload the kegs of black powder and carry them off in three directions.

"Come along," Crocker said. "I'll show you something you won't soon forget."

Crocker led them along the crest of the summit to a prominence of rock that jutted out to the east. "Down there in those trees, you can see my workmen. Some of those kegs of black powder we brought up are going to this eastern portal. Right now, others are being winched down the central shaft. Mr. Strobridge is down there, as you can see."

Jessie nodded. She had already identified tall Harvey Strobridge with his black eye patch. He was obviously directing men to fell trees and move forward on grading a roadbed down the Truckee Canyon toward Reno.

"I'm not waiting to bore under Donner Pass before we begin this section," Crocker explained. "Because the United States Congress provides us with a generous subsidy for every mile of track we lay, it is my intention to immediately begin to lay track down that canyon and across the desert."

"But didn't Congress specify that it had to be *continuous* track?" Jessie asked as the realization of what Crocker had in mind struck her.

"Oh sure," Crocker said, dismissing her objection as if it were nothing. "But by the time the bureaucrats stop arguing about whether or not what this railroad has done is in breach of the contract, we'll have finished the summit tunnel and the issue will be history."

"I see," Jessie said, not entirely approving but admitting that she would have done the same if her back was also to the wall. "And, in truth, I can't blame you."

Crocker stared down from his mountaintop, with the wind whipping his beard and hair. He looked as big and solid as a redwood tree and just as enduring.

"I'm going to make a race out of it yet!" he shouted into the wind. "There are plenty of skeptics who say that the Union Pacific will gobble up Utah and Nevada Territory, but they won't. I'll take Nevada, and damned if I don't believe my men can drive halfway across Utah before this thing is said and done."

Without another word, Crocker turned and marched back along the ridge, following a well-worn footpath until he came to the big summit shaft that led straight down into the mountaintop. Jessie and Ki gathered around the hole, which was about ten feet in diameter. Over the shaft was a huge pole tripod from which hung a massive winch and pulleys with a heavy rope that dangled down into the darkness. Looking into the shaft, Jessie could see a light glowing at the bottom, and along the north and south walls were a pair of heavy iron ladders firmly bolted into the rock.

"How deep is it?" Ki asked.

"About eighty-five feet," Crocker replied. "And it had better be on line with the east and west portals or my surveyors and engineers are going to be shot or hanged."

"I can imagine," Jessie said, realizing that while the man was not serious, it would be a colossal blunder if the central tunnels did not meet exactly with the tunnels being bored inward from the eastern and western portals.

Even as they stared down into the dark hole, they heard the whispered brush of sandals on the south ladder as Chinese ascended from the shaft to emerge into the cold sunlight atop the mountain.

"They always go down the north ladder and come up

the south, for obvious reasons," Crocker explained.

"Of course," Ki said, watching three Chinese emerge from the shaft. Their faces were covered with dust and they looked small and tired. "Could I go down there sometime?"

Crocker frowned. "Whatever for?"

"I'd like to see the tunnel work," Ki said.

Crocker shrugged his heavy shoulders. "You go anytime you want. I'll tell my foremen that you can have the run of the place. What about you, Miss Starbuck?"

"I'll pass," she said, staring into the black hole and faintly hearing the sound of picks tearing out the belly of the mountain, inch by back-breaking inch.

Crocker chuckled. "I feel the same way, Miss Starbuck. I could get down easily enough, but hauling myself out would be an unenviable and probably an impossible chore. Come now, let's get off this mountaintop, and I'll take you inside the western portal, where you can get a good idea of what we are facing up here."

Neither Jessie nor Ki argued. The high, windswept summit offered spectacular vistas in every direction, but it was not a place where anyone would linger. Jessie could only imagine how deep the snow would get and how cold it would become in this place in December and January.

The silent Irish driver was still sitting hunched over in his heavy coat waiting for them when they returned to the buckboard. He looked to be in poor humor and said something under his breath to Crocker that Jessie did not hear. Then he pointed back up the trail toward the shaft.

Crocker was about to respond, but suddenly the rock under their feet shook like jelly, and a giant cloud of smoke and flame swept upward from the summit shaft.

Crocker had been about to help Jessie up into the wagon, but now he whirled and lumbered back up the trail. Ki, then Jessie passed him on the run, and when the samurai arrived back at the shaft, he stood back as a spout of dust and smoke was torn apart by the wind.

Crocker, pale and out of breath, arrived several minutes behind Jessie, and the three of them stood in mute, horrified silence, watching the shaft belch its poison.

"I don't understand it," Crocker mumbled, shaken to his own core. "The Chinese never made a mistake like that before. They have the greatest respect for black powder. We have safety precautions that make it virtually impossible for such a disaster as this to occur. I don't understand!"

"Mr. Crocker," Jessie said, placing her hand on the man's arm and wondering how many Chinese had just been blown to smithereens beneath their feet, "the Union Pacific also had very stringent safety precautions, but explosions kept ripping down their trestles and tunnels. It was sabotage, just as I told you."

Crocker tore his eyes away from the smoky shaft. He looked at Jessie and then at Ki. "You both have my permission to hunt down and destroy whoever is doing these terrible acts! I can't have my men dying by the hands of other men. It's enough that they must die because of this damned mountain!"

Jessie and Ki understood. They stared down into the smoky hole and shivered in the cold, cutting wind.

Chapter 13

As soon as the smoke and dust from the summit shaft explosion cleared enough that they could breathe, Ki volunteered to be the first man down the ladder. He carried a kerosene lantern, and with a handkerchief over his nose and mouth, he made a complete tour of both the east and the west tunnels.

What he saw was complete devastation. The tremendous explosion had blown apart boxes, wheelbarrows and the unfortunate Chinese who had been working the shaft tunnels. Only fragments of bone and cloth remained of the workmen, and it was not a sight for the weak-stomached. Ki hollered up the shaft, instructing those above to drop canvas tarpaulins so that he could wrap up the scattered remains.

He knew the Chinese believed that they could not go to their afterworld unless they were buried in their homeland. Therefore, it was important that their remains be sent back across the ocean for burial.

"Any clue as to what happened?" Crocker asked when Ki emerged from the tunnel, wheezing and choking on the lingering dust and smoke.

"No," the samurai said. "When the air clears, you

might find something, but I doubt it very much. The explosion erased everything and everyone."

"Son of a bitch!" Crocker swore. "The thing I can't understand is how they did it! I mean, anyone who lit the black powder would have been seen emerging from the shaft in a hell of a hurry."

"He didn't emerge," Ki said. "The first thing I looked for when I got back here was footprints. No, whoever lit the fuse blew himself to pieces."

Both Crocker and Jessie blinked, and Jessie recovered first. "Then the man had to have been tricked into thinking he could escape unseen."

"Yes," Ki said. "I think that is the only rational explanation."

Crocker stared at the smoking shaft. "I think that I had better call a work stop and tell the men about our suspicions. Any objections to that?"

"No," Jessie said. "It will mean tipping off our hand, but we need the workmen to be aware that there are enemies in this camp and to watch for them."

"Then that settles it," Crocker said. "I'll call the meeting for this afternoon."

The meeting was held at three o'clock under threatening skies and in the teeth of a hard, gusting wind.

Crocker surveyed his army of Chinese along with several hundred grim-faced foremen and supervisors. His expression was as wintery as the sky, and he wasted no time with preliminaries.

"Men," he said, as his words were rapidly translated into Chinese by an interpreter, "today we had another explosion. This time it was at the foot of the summit shaft, and although no accurate count has yet been taken, we think we lost about twenty good men. Maybe even

107

more. Four or five were Irish or Mexican foremen, and the rest were Chinese—men hand-picked by Mr. Strobridge to work in the shaft tunnels."

Crocker paused and lit a cigar with some difficulty while his workmen absorbed this somber news.

"I would like to think that the summit shaft explosion was an accident—but it wasn't. I think the explosion was the act of a murderer. A man intent on stopping us right here on the summit when victory is finally within our grasp."

Jessie watched the faces of the crews. The Chinese, known for their inscrutability, suddenly became animated. The Irish workers were even more outraged and shocked by this startling news.

Harvey Strobridge raised his long arms for silence. "All right!" he shouted. "You've heard it from the boss man. Now I'm going to add my own opinions, and I want every one of you to listen close before you go back to work."

Strobridge glared at the men and he looked formidable. With his slightly aquiline nose and single glaring eye, he somehow reminded Jessie of a large bird of prey.

"If that explosion was purposefully set, the man who did it never got out of that shaft alive. He was tricked into an act of sabotage that ended his own life. That means that whoever is behind this is a man so dead inside that he would sell out his own mother. We want that man— or men—because we know they will continue to sabotage this railroad until either they win—or this railroad wins."

Strobridge cleared his throat. "So we're asking you to spy on each other. Watch for any unusual behavior. If you see a man go off alone to a place where he ought not be, then we want to hear about it. If you see someone steal black powder or take it without authorization, tell

108

either Mr. Crocker or myself. We want to make damn sure that no one uses explosives unless they are authorized to do so. Is that perfectly clear?"

Thousands of solemn men nodded their heads.

"Then that's it," Crocker said in dismissal. "We are going to be on this mountain until we've punched under this summit and are driving track into Reno. We won't quit until we meet the Union Pacific, and we damn sure don't intend for that to happen until we reach Utah Territory. So let's move!"

When the workmen had dispersed and returned to their labors, Jessie joined Crocker and Strobridge.

"I'm going to San Francisco and find us a chemist to make nitroglycerine," she announced.

"Given what happened today," Crocker said, "don't you think something that unstable would do us more harm than good?"

"No," Jessie said. "Black powder is safer, I'll grant that. But it's too accessible. Anyone can steal a few kegs and use it for their own destructive purposes against this railroad. But if we could substitute it with nitroglycerine, which only one man would formulate and be responsible for, then we could at least have some control over our explosives."

"Good point," Crocker said.

Strobridge agreed, with a nod of his head. "I was sending a supply train back to Sacramento today anyway. From Sacramento you can take a steamer to San Francisco and be there by tomorrow."

"Excellent," Jessie said. "I'll find us a chemist, buy what is necessary to formulate the explosive and return as soon as possible. I might also put my ear to the ground for something to give us a clue as to what we are up against."

"That would help," Strobridge said.

Jessie turned to her samurai. "I want you to remain here and guard Mr. Crocker and Mr. Strobridge. If I were a member of that crowd and part of the sabotage, these two men would be my next targets."

Protest flickered in Ki's brown, almond-shaped eyes, but he said nothing. Besides, Jessie's logic was correct— Crocker and Strobridge were the vital elements in stopping this railroad's progress. Eliminate either one, and it would be an irreparable loss to the Central Pacific. Eliminate them both, and the transcontinental railroad might not be constructed over Donner Pass for decades, if ever.

Just before Jessie boarded the supply train, she took the samurai aside and said, "I want you to protect their lives as if they were me."

"What you ask is impossible," Ki said. "But I will try."

"Good. Don't worry about me. I'm sure that I will return within a week, two weeks at the latest. I hope that I can learn something in San Francisco about what we are facing here. If the ring is an international cartel such as the one that finally killed my father, then San Francisco has to be their West Coast base of operations, and I have many friends of influence there who can be of enormous help to us."

"If you ask too many questions, then your own life will be in great danger," Ki said.

"I will be discreet. And in truth, there isn't much I can do here. But by protecting Mr. Crocker and Mr. Strobridge, you can make all the difference between this railroad's success or failure."

Ki understood, and when he had helped Jessie up onto

the train, he trained his highly disciplined mind to focus on his new and unfamiliar role as the protector of the two brash, outspoken and headstrong railroad builders.

He would do as Jessie asked, but he would rather be at her side.

Chapter 14

When Jessie arrived in San Francisco, she disembarked from the steamer *Houston* and quickly made her way up from the pier into the city. San Francisco felt comfortable and familiar to Jessie because it had played a large part in her childhood. It was here that Alex Starbuck had made his start. Jessie remembered how she and her mother used to walk the steep cobblestone streets and watch the sailing ships come in from around the world.

The smells and sounds of Chinatown were part of her earliest memories, and she remembered the way this great seaport city had boomed during the Forty-Niner gold rush. Overnight, it seemed, San Francisco had turned from a sleepy little seaport into a mecca for fortune seekers and dreamers from around the world.

She remembered her father's laughter and the smell of his pipe. How men from all walks of life had come to him with respect and how his name and picture had often been in the San Francisco papers during the gold rush days.

Funny, Jessie thought, pausing to catch her breath on a steep hill that afforded one of the most spectacular views of the bay, her father had gotten involved in almost everything except the gold fields that had made this town. Jessie knew that while the transcontinental's western terminus was Sacramento, this seaport would still reap enormous benefits. As things stood now, everything from Europe or the East Coast had to be shipped ten thousand miles around Cape Horn, a turbulent and dangerous voyage at any time of the year.

Jessie continued on up the street, aware of the admiring glances she received from the men that she passed. She considered it quite a compliment, considering that she was dressed in the same rough working clothes that she had worn while fleeing Paiute across the Utah and Nevada Territories.

Halfway up the block, Jessie paused outside her father's first office building and fondly recalled the grand opening, which she and her mother had attended. The mayor of San Francisco—a portly Irishman with red cheeks—had said wonderful things about Alex Starbuck, though Jessie had been too young to fully understand the praises.

Jessie touched the weathered brick wall and closed her eyes, remembering that long ago day. A child believes things will never change and that the ones they most love will live forever and ever without pain or sorrow.

"Miss . . . are you all right?"

Jessie opened her eyes to see a kindly old man peering at her with concern.

"Yes," she said. "But thank you for asking."

He smiled and walked slowly on. Jessie inhaled deeply and pulled her fingers away from the monument of her father's success. That was all past now. It seemed a lifetime ago, and the memory was now bittersweet when she thought about how that evil international cartel had finally taken the lives of both her parents.

Ten minutes later, Jessie pushed her way through the

front door of her own office building and entered the lobby with its polished oak floors and woodwork carved by German artists. One glance told her that everything here was running smoothly, but there were too many people working in too small a space. Jessie's West Coast operations had grown so fast that she was now considering a much larger building, one south of town with enough real estate to expand indefinitely.

Her office manager, Gavin Blake, a tall, handsome man in his midthirties, was a graduate of the school of international business at Cornell University. He was in conference in his glass-enclosed office.

A young clerk approached Jessie and said, "Can I be of service, Miss?"

The clerk was more boy than man. Pimply-faced, very formal and polite, he could not have been over seventeen.

"Yes," Jessie said, "I would like to speak to Mr. Blake."

The clerk glanced over his shoulder into the manager's office. He turned back to Jessie. "Do you have an appointment?"

"No," Jessie said, "but. . . . "

"Then I'm afraid Mr. Blake is occupied at the moment. But if you would please have a seat, I will tell him you wish to see him at his earliest convenience, Miss. . . ."

"Starbuck," Jessie said, "Jessica Starbuck."

The clerk's reaction could not have been more dramatic. His jaw dropped and his eyes bulged. He stammered unintelligibly for a moment, then whirled and bolted across the office in a series of great bounds.

Jessie had to stifle a giggle as the clerk burst into Gavin's office and frantically pointed her out to his manager. Gavin himself showed quite a shock as he recognized Jessica and rushed out of his office, leaving his employees without explanation.

"Miss Starbuck!" he cried loud enough for the entire office to be alerted to the fact that their boss was on the premises. "What a wonderful surprise!"

"I'm sure it is," Jessie said, extending her hands in greeting. "I did not wish to interrupt, but. . . . "

"Nonsense!" Gavin exclaimed. "Your accountants, property experts and I were just discussing the acquisition of a new piece of property for our office expansion. As you can see, we're bursting at the seams."

"And have been for quite some time," Jessie said.

"I'll finish our meeting later," Gavin said.

"No, no. I'd like to sit in if you don't mind."

"Of course not. Come on in!"

Jessie was escorted into her manager's office. The other members of the management team here were all familiar to her, and Jessie said, "Please carry on with your discussion. I'll step in if I have any suggestions, though I'm sure that you are all much more qualified to decide on this matter than I am."

After twenty minutes of listening, Jessie made one small suggestion regarding one of the alternative properties being considered, and then she allowed Gavin to finish out the meeting. It was her philosophy to hire the best people and let them run their own show. This style of management had also been her father's, and it had served him very well. Alex, like Jessica, had firmly believed in paying top dollar for top people with only one condition—they had to produce.

When the meeting ended, firm decisions were made regarding which parcel of property to buy as well as the price to be offered and the highest acceptable price that would be paid.

Each of the men excused themselves and left Jessie and Gavin alone.

"Coffee or tea?" he asked.

"Coffee."

They exchanged idle pleasantries, and when the same young clerk had brought them coffee, Gavin closed the door and asked they not be disturbed unless the building was on fire.

When they were assured of privacy, Gavin peered over his coffee cup and said, "You look very serious, Jessica. What is wrong?"

"The Union Pacific Railroad was being sabotaged in Wyoming," she said without preamble. "Ki and I were able to stop the ringleader, but we never learned who masterminded the effort. Now, we've just left the Central Pacific at Donner Summit, and they have the same kind of problems."

Gavin sat up straighter in his chair, coffee forgotten. "Do you suspect anyone?"

"I am leaning toward the theory that foreign interests wish to see the transcontinental fail, so that it can be rerouted south, through northern Mexico."

"But why?"

"Mexico is in a state of revolution again," Jessie said. "The leader of the revolutionists is a man named Juarez. He is openly seeking foreign guns and foreign money. I'm sure that, in return, there are promises."

"Such as?"

"Such as," Jessie explained, "if Juarez were to overthrow his government and become president of his country, he would be in a position to strike any kind of railroad deal. He could make building a transcontinental railroad extremely profitable. He could use Mexican prisoners by the thousand and give land subsidies to foreign interests that would make the United States Congress's subsidies seem paltry by comparison."

Gavin shook his head. "I take it this is all speculation at this point?"

"Yes," Jessie admitted. "But consider how much sense it makes. A Mexican revolutionist with control of the army could promise an international cartel that he would help them finance and build a railroad, from the Texas border at the Gulf of Mexico to the Pacific Ocean at the California border, that would offer shipping rates so cheap they would bankrupt an American competitor."

Jessie finished her coffee and came to her feet. "I'll be staying in town only long enough to make some discreet inquiries. If foreigners are behind the grand plot I've outlined, then perhaps they've dropped a word here and there in an effort to recruit men of influence and money into their camp."

"It sounds dangerous," Gavin said. "I would like you to know that I'm at your service day . . . or night."

Jessie smiled at his double meaning. She and Gavin had once been lovers. "Perhaps I could use a little help."

He beamed. "May I call on you for dinner?"

"Not tonight," Jessie said. "As you can see by my dress and appearance, I'm tired and need to go to bed early. Without being obvious, ask a few questions on your own. You know the people in this town better than I. Make your own inquiries and then, tomorrow evening, come by, and we will go to dinner and compare notes."

Gavin nodded. "I will do everything possible to bring this matter to a rapid conclusion."

"Good." Jessie started to leave, but hesitated at the door. "You wouldn't . . . No, I'm sure you wouldn't," she said, going out the door.

117

"Wouldn't what?"

"Know any chemists willing to take great risks for great rewards."

"Chemists?"

Jessie smiled. "See, I told you you wouldn't."

And then she left.

Chapter 15

Jessie and Ki always stayed at San Francisco's old Heritage Hotel. The imposing four-story edifice was constructed of sandstone and was of gothic design with elegant marble floors in the lobby and a chandelier from Italy that Jessica thought was utterly magnificent.

The moment Jessie walked into the stately hotel, she was fawned over and escorted to the best available suite, one with a view overlooking the great San Francisco Bay. Because she was a regular guest, it was not necessary for her to register or even to send her clothes out for cleaning, because the hotel kept a duplication of her complete wardrobe under lock and key.

"Welcome back, Miss Starbuck!" the hotel manager gushed effusively as he entered her room carrying a huge floral bouquet, which he centered on a sixteenth-century French pedestal. "We are delighted to see you after such a long absence."

"I have been quite busy," she conceded.

"And where is Mr. Ki today?"

"He is in the Sierras," Jessie said, realizing that this was the first time that she had ever been here without the samurai. "A matter of some urgency keeps him away."

"I see, I see," the manager said, bowing and grinning broadly. "Well, a bath?"

"Yes," Jessie said as two bellboys hurried in pushing a clothes hanger on wheels, on which hung her wardrobe. "It would be very much appreciated."

"And what about supper?"

"I will eat downstairs in the dining room. My usual favorite, chicken with shrimp and curry, please."

"Will you be in the company of a gentleman?"

"I don't think so," she said.

"Very good, Miss Starbuck," the manager said, shooing the bellboys out the moment they had transferred Jessie's wardrobe into her cedar closets. "Very good indeed, and we will be sending up the usual bottle of French champagne on ice, compliments of the Heritage!"

Twenty minutes later, Jessie was soaking in a bubble bath and sipping champagne and feeling very relaxed.

That night, she did eat alone, in a very private section of the hotel dining room. After dinner, she retired for the night, and the soft bed, clean silk sheets and feather pillow all conspired to give her a refreshing night's sleep.

By nine o'clock the next morning, Jessie was on the street and instructing one of the city's horse carriages to drive her up California Street to Kearney, where she ordered the driver to stop.

"Driver, that carriage behind us, wasn't it the same one that was waiting for a fare behind you at the Heritage?"

The driver turned around and studied the carriage in question. "I . . . I don't know," he said. "I never pay any attention what's behind, only to what's ahead. But it's not likely, miss."

Jessie glanced again at the carriage. The driver had a

120

bored expression on his face and seemed to be waiting for another fare. Jessie could not see inside the carriage and could not tell if it was occupied or not.

She dismissed her concern as being unimportant. Why would anyone follow her?

She consulted the address she had written down and then studied the building before her with more than a casual interest, especially the defaced sign, which she could barely decipher to read: Bowden Chemical Company.

"This *must* be Dr. James Bowden's offices, although it looks practically deserted."

"Bowden?" The driver frowned. "The name sounds familiar. Is he famous or something?"

"Infamous, I'm afraid. Dr. Bowden is the experimental chemist who was suspected of formulating the nitroglycerine that leveled that city block we passed a few minutes ago."

"Oh, it's him you're after, is it!" The driver, a slim, dapper man wearing a bowler hat, black overcoat and matching gloves, suddenly grew quite animated and upset. "I lost one of my best friends in that explosion. He was drivin' his cab past the building when it exploded. Damn shame it was. Left a wife and three fine children!"

"I'm sorry to hear that," Jessie said, paying the angry driver. "I heard about the explosion and knew Dr. Bowden was in jail for quite some time. But it is my understanding that someone unauthorized stole his chemicals, and then they must have dropped or shaken them, and the nitroglycerine exploded."

"Ahh!" the driver snapped with derision. "That's a bunch of poppycock to my way of thinking! They never found a suspect, so there's no proof of theft."

"But how could there be if the thief was blown to smithereens?" Jessie asked.

The driver ignored her question. He wasn't going to change his mind about Bowden no matter what facts got in the way of his conclusions.

"Miss," he said in a voice shaking with anger, "the only thing anyone can say for sure is that Bowden brewed that damn glycerine, and he's the one that's the cause of a lot of innocent people getting blown to bits!"

Jessie saw no point in discussing the matter further. It was clear from this man's anger, and from the outraged newspaper columns she'd read, that Bowden was probably San Francisco's least popular citizen.

Jessie paid the driver and entered the rundown building. At first, she thought that it was abandoned. There was a handwritten sign on the inside door that read, Bowden Chemical Company Closed. Go Away.

Jessie had no intention of going away. When the nitroglycerine explosion and resulting tragedy had occurred, the affair and the tremendous public outrage it created had been reported worldwide. Nitroglycerine was said to be ten times more powerful than black powder but so unstable as to be almost impossible to use. The newspapers reported that explosives researchers were working on a new form of nitroglycerine in a powder base that was much safer but every bit as powerful.

However, for now, the dangerous yellow liquid was the only hope that Jessie could see for pushing the long summit tunnel under Donner Pass by next spring. And Dr. Bowden, said to be brilliant, eccentric and reclusive, was supposed to be the foremost authority on nitroglycerine west of the Mississippi River.

"Hello!" Jessie called, knocking on the door.

She thought she heard a sound and turned the doorknob. It was unlocked, but when she attempted to push it open, she suddenly realized that there was someone preventing her from doing so on the other side.

"Dr. Bowden?"

"Go away!" he said in a high-pitched voice. "Dr. Bowden is not here anymore. Go away!"

Jessie had managed to get her foot in the door, and she was not about to go away until she at least had a chance to speak to the reclusive chemist. "I know it's you, Dr. Bowden. Open up—we need to talk!"

"I'm not Dr. Bowden! Now go away or so help me I'll . . . I'll shoot you with the gun I have in my hand."

Jessie did not believe the man for a single moment, but that did not help her to open the door.

"Dr. Bowden," she grunted, pushing as hard as she could, "this is ridiculous. I didn't come to condemn you. I know that the accident was not your fault. How could you be responsible for the act of a thief?"

"That's what I kept asking the authorities!" Bowden cried. "But it didn't keep me out of jail. Or save my professional reputation or business. I'm ruined. I'm vilified. I'm an outcast!"

Jessie heard pain and humiliation in the man's voice. "I want to hire you," she said.

The pressure behind the door eased a fraction. "What did you say?"

"I'll pay you ten dollars a day." That was undoubtedly more money than even Harvey Strobridge was earning.

"Ten dollars! For what?"

"Dr. Bowden," Jessie said, "I'm not going to stand here and discuss a job offer while we hold this door up! Now let me in and we can talk."

There was a long pause, and then Bowden reluctantly opened the door. Jessie beheld a slight, ruffled man in his fifties with thick glasses, unruly hair and a weak chin.

His clothes were threadbare; he wore a dirty apron and his sleeves were rolled up to his skinny biceps. Jessie also noted that his fingernails were chewed to the quick and his hands were stained yellow.

Behind the scientist was a complete laboratory, though it was one in a state of disarray, like the man himself.

"Who are you?" he demanded, staring myopically at her through his thick lenses.

"My name is Jessica Starbuck. On an unofficial basis, I am representing the Central Pacific Railroad. The railroad is not making very good progress at its summit tunnel under Donner Pass."

"What has that to do with me?"

"A great deal," Jessie said. "I want you to come to the Sierras and help them blow a tunnel under the summit."

The scientist's eyes widened. "Me? In the mountains? You must be mad! I would freeze up there. Be eaten by bears. Fall off a cliff. Get lost and never be found. You must be mad!"

"No," Jessie said in her calmest voice. "I would see that you were very safe and that all your physical needs were met. That you had a servant to help you and even a cabin for your privacy and for working on your experiments, and that ten dollars a day was deposited in your account or paid to you in gold."

Bowden swallowed. He shook his head as if distracted and turned to shuffle back into his laboratory, giving himself a few moments to adjust to this astounding offer.

"Just look at my laboratory," he whispered. "It is chaos, like my life! Since the explosion and my jail sentence, everything I've ever done has been held up to ridicule."

"I am sorry about that," Jessie said. "But if that is

so, then what I am offering you is even more important than money. It's the chance to do something for the good of this country. It's an opportunity to show people that nitroglycerine, and Dr. James Bowden, can make a *positive* contribution to society. This country desperately *needs* the transcontinental railroad. Without your help, it may not get it."

Dr. Bowden removed his soiled laboratory apron and slumped down on a stool, oblivious for a moment of Jessie and everything else surrounding him.

Jessie walked over to a bubbling flask and sniffed at some awful chemical mixture, then moved quietly to the lone, grimy window and stared out at the street for a moment before she turned around.

"Well, Doctor? Are you going to seize the opportunity to regain your finances as well as your reputation, or are you going to remain here, locked up in this 'chaos,' as you call it, bitter and defeated?"

The scientist slowly lifted his head. He rubbed his weak chin thoughtfully, then removed his thick glasses and massaged his watery eyes with his thumb.

"You have a very convincing way with words, Miss Starbuck. But I am a very reclusive soul who cannot tolerate excitement. The humiliation of being locked in a filthy jail, the vilifying and unfair publicity I received, the courtroom hearing to determine if I was a mass murderer . . . all those things were a nightmare I keep reliving."

Jessie walked over to the scientist and placed her hand on his thin shoulder.

"I understand," she said in a gentle voice. "Who is to say why some thief would be stupid enough to break into a laboratory and steal chemicals? Maybe it was simply a drunkard hoping to sell your flasks or some of this laboratory equipment. Perhaps—God forbid—it was some gang of youths stealing for thrills. I guess the answer will never be known. But that doesn't matter now. What matters is that you can have a second chance, on the Central Pacific Railroad. You can redeem your reputation in the eyes of this country."

"Yes," he said, raising his chin a little. "Yes, I suppose I can at that."

Jessie squeezed his shoulder. "Everything you need will be transported with us to Sacramento by steamer and then by the Central Pacific to Donner Summit. Will it be safe?"

"Of course. There is no danger until the elements of nitroglycerine are combined. No danger whatsoever."

"Good! How soon can you pack the necessary chemicals and be ready to leave?"

"Two weeks?"

"Much too long," Jessie said. "Three days at the most."

Bowden looked as if he were going to change his mind, so Jessie said, "All right, next Monday I will arrive with a wagon to transport us and your necessary supplies. That gives you five days. Can you do it?"

"If I must, then yes."

Jessie breathed a sigh of relief. If Dr. Bowden had refused to help, she would have been forced to send a telegram back to the East requesting another scientist whose expertise was explosives. There weren't many, and with Bowden's agreement to help, things would be greatly speeded up.

"Next Monday then," she said.

She started toward the door, but Bowden cleared his throat and said, "Miss Starbuck?"

"Yes?"

"I will need to buy crates and packing materials. And I have no warm clothes for winter. I. . . . "

"How thoughtless of me!" Jessie exclaimed, hurrying back to the man and reaching into her purse, from which she extracted two hundred dollars.

Bowden looked at the money as if he had not seen any in a long time. And, Jessie thought, the poor man probably hadn't, because the tragic explosion had branded him a pariah in this community and driven his business into the ground.

"This will have to come out of my salary so. . . . "

"No, Doctor" Jessie said, "this is expense money. I will be reimbursed by the Central Pacific at some later date, I'm sure."

Bowden actually managed a smile. "Thank you very, very much," he whispered.

Jessie nodded and left the scientist to the important work of shutting down his laboratory and preparing to go to the Sierras. She had met men like Bowden before. They were gentle, naive and helpless, very often the dearest of men, really, childlike in so many ways.

And as for her two hundred dollars, well, she would not submit it to the Central Pacific. They had money troubles of their own. And besides, when their accountants learned what they were paying the eccentric chemist to concoct and administer his potent brew to the insides of the Summit Tunnel, they would probably blow up too.

Outside, her cab was still waiting as she had instructed. But most disturbing, so was the cab that she had earlier noted.

"I think I need some fresh air and to see the sights of this town again," Jessie said, wanting to learn if the carriage behind them was, indeed, following her.

"What would you like to see first?" her driver asked.

"Oh, why don't we drive up to the old Spanish presidio for a starter. It's a magnificent view of the bay from there, don't you think?"

The driver shrugged. "Did you see that crazy Bowden?"

"I did."

"I hope you gave him a piece of your mind. Damn crazy fool!"

"Oh, he's not so bad," Jessie said, allowing herself to be assisted up into the carriage.

When it drove away, she looked back and, sure enough, they were being followed. But to be absolutely sure would require a few more miles.

Jessie settled back in the dim recesses of the carriage. Who would follow her? The same people that were sabotaging the Central Pacific?

Who else indeed?

Jessie reached into her purse and checked the two-shot derringer she carried, to make sure that it was loaded and ready to use. It was, so she slipped it up her sleeve and supposed she was ready for whatever the rest of the day would bring.

★

Chapter 16

By the time that Jessie arrived at the old Spanish presidio, she was absolutely certain that she was being followed. The driver of her carriage stopped beside a winding dirt road and dismounted to open the door.

"Here we are," he said. "Best view of the bay is right over there."

Jessie glanced back at the coach that was following them. She pretended she did not know she was being shadowed, in the hope that she might be able to learn the identities of her enemies. Her derringer was loaded and stuffed up her silk sleeve, ready to use in an instant should the need arise.

"Over there?" she asked.

"Yes," the driver said in a curt voice. "Right at the edge."

Jessie felt the hair on the back of her neck prickle in warning. She did not like or even trust her driver. The coach that was following her passed them and disappeared over a small hill, so that it was lost from view.

Jessie took a deep breath and tried to look calm and relaxed. She strolled to the edge of the cliff. It was straight down for almost three hundred feet to some rocks below.

Jessie's driver, however, had not been exaggerating, the view was nothing less than spectacular. She could see almost the entire bay, with its several large and rocky islands, which were often shrouded in low, coastal fog. The water was a deep green and dotted with merchant ships from all nations. Hundreds of sea gulls wheeled and effortlessly rode the thermal updrafts that caromed off the cliffs.

"It's magnificent," Jessie said to her driver, her voice carefree but her heart pounding with anxiety. "Did you know that the Spaniards passed the narrow mouth of this great harbor for almost two hundred years before they came across it?"

"Must have been blind," the driver said.

"I don't know, the. . . ."

Jessie didn't have time to finish because the driver suddenly lunged at her with his outstretched hands, clearly intent on shoving her off the cliff. The attack caught Jessie by surprise; she had expected trouble from someone in the coach that had been following her, not from her own driver.

Jessie did not have time to turn or run or even to palm her derringer. The only thing she could do was to drop to her hands and knees.

The driver's momentum propelled him forward, and he could not check himself before his knees struck Jessie in the side.

"Ahhh!" he shouted in horror, his arms windmilling crazily as he flew headlong over the side. Jessie heard him screaming all the way down the cliff. When his body struck the first rocks that jutted out below, it ricocheted back into the air, spun like a rag doll another seventy or eighty feet and then disappeared into heavy brush.

Jessie rose to her feet and peered over the edge. She

130

shuddered and pivoted toward her carriage with every intention of leaving as fast as possible. Clearly, her enemies were out to kill her.

She raced for her carriage, but before she could reach it, two gunmen appeared and one fired a shot that could not have missed her by more than a few inches. Jessie swore in frustration, turned and ran along the edge of the sea cliff, desperately searching for an avenue of escape.

Another bullet propelled her ahead. Her long, shapely legs churned, and she was an excellent runner. She turned away from the cliff and tried to angle back toward the presidio, certain that she would find help there. A horseman burst into view with a rope in his hand and came galloping toward her.

Jessie had no choice but to turn back toward the cliff. The horseman was gaining extremely fast, and she knew he would overtake her in a few moments.

There was no escape here. She kept peering over the edge of the cliff, hoping that she might see a path down toward the bay. When she realized the futility of her efforts and the drumming hoofbeats sounded as if they were right behind her, Jessie whirled, aimed her derringer and fired at almost point-blank range.

The horseman, whose rope was now twirling overhead, took the .38-caliber bullet in the chest. His rope spilled across the grass, and he made a pathetic attempt with his hands to plug the crimson leak that was emptying away his life.

"Damn you!" he raged with his dying breath as he tumbled from his horse.

The horse was badly frightened by the gunfire that had erupted almost in its face. It shied away, and Jessie threw herself at the trailing reins. She managed to grab them and jerk the horse to a standstill. With a strength born of desperation, she grabbed the saddlehorn and vaulted into the saddle. The horse needed no urging and ran, as bullets pursued them with a vengeance.

Jessie pulled the horse up behind a tree and reloaded her derringer. She could hear bullets striking the bark of the tree and knocking off leaves and branches, but she held her horse steady with one hand and finished reloading her derringer.

When she looked up, she had what she wanted, a good look at the faces of her enemies. There were three men, all dark complected and already out of breath from running. The man in the center was the largest, and Jessie had an instant impression that he was the leader. He was in his late thirties, heavyset with thick features. His two companions were smaller, both whippetlike and quite thin.

A bullet whipped past Jessie's face, and she aimed her derringer at the leader and fired. She missed, as she knew she would given that her horse was jumping all over the place and the derringer was not a weapon of great accuracy beyond ten or fifteen yards.

The three men dove to the grass, and Jessie fired once more before she wheeled her horse around and drove her heels into its sides. The animal burst into a run and left the remaining gunmen far behind.

Jessie galloped back into town with only one thought in mind. She had to get the reclusive Dr. Bowden out of San Francisco in a hurry before the men who had tried to kill her could find them. Too late, Jessie realized that whoever had been following her would have realized she was visiting an explosives expert, and it would not have been difficult to guess the purpose of her unannounced call.

"I just hope they haven't killed him already," Jessie said. "I should never have left the poor, defenseless man alone."

Wearing a dress on horseback caused a lot of heads to turn as Jessie frantically weaved her way through the heavy wagon traffic that clogged many of San Francisco's busiest streets. By the time she reached the Bowden Chemical Company, her horse was in a lather and soaking wet. Jessie tied the out-of-breath animal at a hitch post and quickly reloaded the derringer before darting toward the building's front entrance.

The front door was ajar and Jessie heard angry voices inside. She forced herself to go slowly as she tiptoed into the building with the derringer raised and ready to fire.

"For the last time!" the angry voice cried. "What did the Starbuck woman tell you she wanted?"

"Nothing!" Bowden said in a voice more angry than frightened. "And for the last time—you are trespassing on private property!"

Jessie heard the sharp retort of flesh striking flesh. She stepped out in the open to see a short but extremely powerful-looking man holding and slapping Bowden while a second man watched with a gun in his fist.

"Hold it right there!" Jessie shouted. "Drop the gun!"

All three were caught by surprise, but Dr. Bowden reacted first and collapsed to the floor like a dead weight. The man with the gun saw he was up against a woman with only a derringer, and he turned to fire, but Jessie's bullet knocked him backward. He slid down the wall, his face a picture of disbelief until the moment he died.

"Freeze!" Jessie cried to the second killer. "I've already drilled a couple of your friends with this derringer. And I've got one more bullet with your name on it."

The powerful man froze.

"Raise your hands," Jessie ordered. "Now!"

Dr. Bowden jumped up from the floor, and to Jessie's

complete amazement, he slapped the gorilla-strong thug twice across the face—hard.

"Dr. Bowden, get whatever you need to make nitro-glycerine. We're leaving before more unwanted company arrives."

Jessie had expected a protest from the scientist, but none was offered as Bowden began to race about his laboratory, grabbing flasks and solutions and jamming them in a wooden box.

"Take it easy!" the thug cried. "You'll blow us all to pieces!"

"No I won't," Bowden said. "Not unless the chemicals are mixed."

The explosives expert grinned maliciously. "Of course, if your other friends were to come by and make trouble, I could mix a yellow brew that would start things off with a real bang. Even a single vial would be enough."

Jessie could not help but react with a smile of grim amusement. Bowden, it seemed, operated best under pressure, and rather than be intimidated by the physical abuse he'd just received, the scientist seemed to have reacted with anger and a good deal of backbone.

Jessie said, "Who hired you and your late friend to come here?"

In reply the thug's lips curled in contempt, and he hissed, "I don't know what the hell you are talking about, lady. I wasn't hired by anyone. Me and my friend saw this laboratory and figured it would be easy to break into. We thought we might be able to steal something valuable enough to sell for whiskey. But once we were inside, this mad scientist found us and went crazy. I grabbed and slapped him a few times, trying to knock some sense into him."

134

"I don't believe you," Jessie said. "I am certain that whoever you work for is responsible for the sabotage at Donner Pass."

" 'Sabotage'? What the hell are you talking about? Me and friend are just thieves. So take me to jail!"

Jessie cocked the derringer. "For the last time, who are you and who hired you? I know you work for people who are trying to stop the building of the transcontinental railroad by any means possible. Who are they!"

The man swallowed and sweat began to bead his forehead. "Hey, lady, I know you can shoot straight. My partner learned that the hard way. But I can't tell you anything."

Jessie raised the pistol and pretended she was going to execute the man if he did not talk. "We can't afford to let you live. Say your prayers."

"No, wait! I'll talk! Just don't shoot!"

Jessie lowered the gun just a fraction. "I'm listening. But I want names."

"Roland Cross," the man growled. "The leader's name is Cross!"

"Where is he?"

"I don't know! I've never seen him. I don't even know what he looks like. I just overheard someone drop his name. If they knew I'd heard it, they'd probably kill me."

"More names!"

"Guito. Don't know his last name. I met him though. He's the man that paid us."

"What does he look like?"

"Big guy, dark complected. Black hair and. . . ."

It was the man that Jessie had missed with her derringer out at the presidio. "He had two smaller guys," she said quickly. "Both of them also dark. Their names, hurry!"

135

"Vinny and Nick."

"Why are they trying to stop the railroad?"

"I don't know."

Jessie raised her gun and took a deep steadying breath. The man wiped a cold sweat from his face. "Please! Don't kill me. I don't know anything more. We were just following orders. That's all."

Jessie glanced over at the scientist, who had stopped and was now staring at her in morbid fascination, no doubt wondering if she was going to kill the man or not.

"I don't think you should shoot him," Bowden said. "Miss Starbuck, you can't. . . ."

Jessie heard a man shout from the street, and the voice was the same she'd heard beside the cliff.

"Dr. Bowden, they're here already!" she cried. "We've got to get out fast!"

"What about me?" the thug bellowed.

"Run for it!" Jessie ordered.

The man did not have to be told twice. He raced for the front door, flung it open and was instantly cut down in a hail of gunfire.

Jessie helped lift the heavy box of chemicals. "I sure hope you have a back door, Doctor."

"I do," he grunted, pulling the box from her grasp. "I can handle this more safely by myself. You lead the way!"

Jessie flung the door open and bolted out into an alley. At least here was a chance of escape.

"This way," she cried, with Bowden struggling to keep up.

The alley was dim and filled with rotting trash, empty bottles and other debris that made the footing tricky. A cat screeched and flew ahead of Jessie to disappear through a broken board fence. As soon as Jessie and Bowden reached an avenue, between a pair of buildings, that would offer them a chance to escape to the main street, Jessie stopped for the scientist. "You go on! I'll hold them back for a few moments to give you enough time to disappear into the crowd."

"But where?"

"Go right toward Market Street and my offices. If I don't overtake you first, go inside and insist on seeing my manager, Mr. Gavin Blake. Tell him that I'm in trouble and will be along as soon as I can. Stay with him until he can help us both get out of San Francisco!"

"But. . . ."

Jessie saw gunmen burst out of Bowden's chemical factory into the alley. "Go on, hurry!"

The scientist genuinely did not want to abandon Jessie to the killers that were now fanning out in both directions in the alley. Bowden was certain that Jessie would not last five minutes alone against so many.

"Here!" he said, pulling a vial encased in a wad of cotton out of his pocket.

"Is it . . . ?"

"Yes," the scientist said, "it's nitroglycerine. Don't be close to where it lands after you throw it."

Jessie nodded with understanding. There could not have been more than eight ounces of the yellow liquid, and yet its reputation was so bad that she wondered how much damage even such a small quantity would do to the men and the alley.

"Go on!" Jessie whispered. "Run!"

Bowden picked up the box of chemicals and laboratory paraphernalia and went scrambling up the corridor of light that filtered between the two tall buildings. Jessie listened to his retreating footsteps, and then she turned to face the men that were coming to kill her.

"Hey!" she shouted. "I'm waiting down here!"

The hunters formed like a pack of dogs and came running. Jessie fired both rounds of her derringer into the moving mass. One of the killers grunted with pain and skidded in the dirt. The others scattered and began to return fire. Jessie ducked back around the corner as bullets ate into the brick building.

She removed the cotton wadding from around the vial. Her hand shook a little as she raised and cocked it, thinking that she would have to make a smooth throwing motion or the explosive might go off in her own hand.

She took a deep breath. "Here goes," she whispered to herself.

Jessie leaned back out into the alley and hurled the vial with a long throw using all of her strength. Before the vial struck the ground and shattered, Jessie threw herself backward and covered her ears as the explosion ripped through the alley. She felt the brick building she was leaning up against actually rock on its foundation, and a wall of air and flying debris swept past her like a tornado.

"My God!" she breathed. "That's incredible!"

Jessie turned and fled up the alley toward the street. She had no doubt she would quickly overtake Bowden. They would then both go to her offices and find the help they'd need to get safely out of this town.

When she reached the street, she turned right and hurried after the scientist, thinking that she would have died in the alley without that vial of nitroglycerine. As it was, things had worked out better than she might have hoped. She had come to San Francisco determined to bring Bowden to Donner Pass and, hopefully, to uncover something about the saboteurs.

She'd been completely successful with Bowden, and there was little doubt, judging from the explosion she

138

had just witnessed, that nitroglycerine was going to be the salvation of the Central Pacific as it bored its way through the great summit tunnel.

Jessie had never claimed to be an explosives expert, but it seemed to her that the nitroglycerine was more than ten times as powerful as dynamite. Much more. Its power was simply awesome, incomprehensible to anyone who had not seen it first-hand. When Crocker and Strobridge realized what the yellow liquid could do to a mountain, they would use it constantly if a way could be found to control its immense power.

Jessie wondered if Dr. Bowden was man enough to face the constant danger he would have to live with at Donner Summit. Of course, he would have a cabin far removed from the rest of the camp for obvious reasons of safety. Bowden would have to live alone, mixing his yellow brew like some mad Merlin in a castle tower.

In addition to the constant threat of blowing himself up in a mishap or even just while carrying the nitroglycerine from his cabin to the detonation sight, he would be a prime target for the enemies of the Central Pacific Railroad. Enemies that would know that Dr. Bowden just might be the key that would spell the difference between success and failure at the summit tunnel.

Jessie hurried along, glancing back constantly, to see if any of her pursuers had survived the alley blast, and knowing in her heart that they had not.

She thought of Cross and Guito. Two names that meant nothing to her—yet. But they would, and hopefully the samurai was also fitting a few pieces of the puzzle together.

Jessie caught up with the scientist, who was white with exertion. "Thank heavens you are all right!" Bowden exclaimed.

139

Jessie took the box from the man and smiled. "Boy," she said, "when you make a brew, you really don't mess around!"

"It's incredible, isn't it?" the scientist said.

"That's an understatement. Can you use it to beat Donner Pass?"

"I don't know," Bowden admitted. "But since I am now certainly finished in this town, I suppose I have no choice but to find out."

"I'm afraid that is exactly the case, Doctor. I don't yet know what the Central Pacific Railroad is up against, but I can tell you one thing—your life wouldn't be worth a cent if you remained another day in this town."

"I shall miss it terribly," Bowden said. "But I should miss living much more."

Chapter 17

The first blizzard to strike Donner Summit came in late October, but by then, Dr. Bowden and his nitroglycerine were already making a dramatic impact on the progress of the summit tunnel. Each day, the scientist would emerge from his special cabin atop the summit and, escorted by a pair of riflemen to protect against any saboteurs, climb to the summit tunnel shaft.

Having placed two vials of nitroglycerine and two carefully measured quantities of black powder into a special canvas pouch he had fashioned for himself, Bowden would slowly descend the ladder. The riflemen, always nervous because of the fear of being ambushed or having Bowden slip and fall, thus blowing himself and perhaps them to pieces, would stay fifty feet back, as if Bowden had the plague.

No one ever accompanied the scientist down into the shaft to watch, but Bowden thought it important to explain his procedure.

"If I have an accident or am ambushed while carrying nitroglycerine on my person, I will fall and you will never find the pieces of me. Therefore, it is important that you know how to proceed on your own. I have written down the proper way to mix the stable ingredients, which I have in sufficient quantity to turn this mountaintop into a cloud of dust."

"Let's hope that isn't necessary," Strobridge said without humor. "We've got a lot of time and money already invested in the summit tunnel. And frankly, the snow is so deep up here in wintertime that even if a locomotive could pull the grade over the summit, the tracks would be impossible to keep clear during winter."

"I understand perfectly," the scientist said. "I was merely using a figure of speech. Now, I will show you how to explode the nitroglycerine, so watch carefully."

From his pouch, he took a vial of clear liquid and a thimble-sized package wrapped in white linen and said, "Using this vial of water and a mock detonating package of black powder complete with fuse, I will demonstrate."

Jessie, Ki, Strobridge and Crocker all watched as Bowden carefully removed the vial and then placed it in a drill hole made by the Chinese.

"The hole should be large enough for the nitroglycerine as well as the packet of black powder. You simply light the fuse to the black powder, and when it explodes beside the nitroglycerine, it creates a chain reaction."

"I see," Strobridge said with great interest. "So you have the combined power of both explosives."

"Yes, though the black powder's impact is minimal compared to the effect of the nitroglycerine. The trick, of course, is to set the fuses at each working face off the summit shaft so that they explode simultaneously."

"Now that," Crocker said, "sounds pretty difficult."

"It is," Bowden admitted. "I have had to light and clock with a stopwatch perhaps a hundred feet of fuse to get the timing down perfectly."

Jessie cleared her throat. "And what if it *wasn't* perfect? Wouldn't the first explosion create enough of a jarring effect to set off the other explosion at the opposite end of the shaft?"

Bowden shrugged his shoulders. "We can only speculate. My guess is that it might, and there is always the chance that flying shards of rock would strike the second vial and explode it on impact. But I would not want to have to go down into the shaft with only one side detonated and the other perhaps ready to go off at the very next moment."

They nodded, and Ki said, "And we can assume you do this same thing each morning on both the eastern and western portals."

"Exactly," Bowden stomped his feet in the snow. "Of course, with the eastern and western portals, there is no need to coordinate the explosions."

"I'll say one thing," Strobridge commented, "nitroglycerine has been a savior to this tunneling effort. With every black powder explosion we'd been using before, we had to wait a couple of hours just for the smoke to clear. This stuff being smokeless has been a huge help, not to mention the fact that it's so damn much more powerful."

"Exactly," Crocker said. "At the rate we are going, if there are not more 'mishaps,' we should break through under the summit tunnel by January and be off this damned mountain by the beginning of March. My surveyors and trestle men are already working on the Truckee Canyon problems."

"Do you still intend to build snowsheds all along the eastern slopes?" Jessie asked.

Crocker looked to Strobridge, who was the only real engineer and builder among them. "You bet we do. The

143

sheds will be sloped down into the canyon so that the snow will keep sliding off instead of getting to a depth and weight where it'd collapse the heaviest timber we could use to construct those sheds."

"I suppose it will take a lot of timber," Jessie said.

"We have a lot of timber all around us, and even though the Comstock Lode has stripped some of the eastern slopes, running short of timber is not a real concern. We're going to start building the sheds in two weeks, and the grading crews have almost completed our new roadbed all the way down along the Truckee River into Reno."

Crocker had a smile on his face. "I'm going to tell them about our latest decision, Harvey. They'll know about it tomorrow just like the rest of the country."

"What are you talking about?" Ki asked.

"Well," Crocker said, "the *big* news is that Harvey and I have decided to take a locomotive and some construction cars over the summit on sleds."

"What?"

"You heard him," Strobridge said. "With a train operating over on the eastern slopes, we can move the track along fast and build those snowsheds in a hell of a hurry. As it is now, every rail would have to be hauled over the summit by teams of men on snowshoes or maybe horses and mules—if they could beat down a trail."

"But a locomotive!" Jessie exclaimed. "Is that possible? It sounds as awesome a feat as when Hannibal crossed the Alps with his army long ago."

"Not quite that bad. At least we don't have any elephants to feed," Strobridge said. "But yes, it is possible. Mr. Crocker and I have been talking about it for months, and I've had a couple of men down at the roundhouse station in Sacramento learning how to

144

dismantle a locomotive and cars. They've just done it, and the pieces will be arriving up here any day now."

"What about Congress?" Jessie asked. "Seems to me that they might strenuously object to paying you subsidies for track laid eastward out of Reno before you've beaten Donner Summit."

"No doubt," Crocker said, not looking as if he gave a damn. "We are certain that our Washington politicians will be outraged by our ploy to move ahead while we continue to wage warfare on the summit tunnel. But who cares! Let them argue and bluster, then threaten to cut us off without funds! By the time they really get around to passing a binding resolution that could hurt us, it will be spring and Dr. Bowden's nitroglycerine will have carried us all the way under the summit."

Jessie and Ki exchanged glances, and then Jessie said, "All right, so how can we help?"

"Watch for any sign of trouble," Strobridge said. "We expect that it will happen while we're all busting our britches trying to get the main structure of the locomotive over the summit without a mishap. You can just imagine how it would upset our plans if we failed and the locomotive sleds were sabotaged."

"Yes," Jessie said. "And that would be the time that an enemy would find this railroad most vulnerable."

"That's why," Crocker said, "this whole dismantling thing has been so secret. But tomorrow, when that dismantled locomotive and those cars start up this way from Sacramento, there's no way that we can hide our intentions. It's bound to attract plenty of attention."

"Maybe we should go down there today and ride back up with the dismantled parts," Jessie said, looking at Ki. "Someone might even try to derail that supply train before it reaches us."

145

"That's a possibility," Crocker conceded, suddenly looking quite worried. "But I can't ask you to do anything. You'll have to make your own minds up on that. There is a supply train going down to Sacramento within the hour."

Jessie turned to Ki. "We'll be on it and ready for trouble if it comes."

Bowden sniffled and stomped his feet in the snow. "Looks like another storm coming in tonight."

They all studied the sky. Jessie could see that the scientist was probably right. Heavy storm clouds were pushing in from the west and stacking up against the Sierra peaks. The temperature was below freezing, and a stiff wind was whipping the tree branches high overhead.

The Chinese were dressed in heavy woolens with boots and gloves. But as Jessie watched them work, she noted suffering pinched into their thin faces. These hardy Celestials seemed to adapt well to hot weather, but the intense mountain cold bothered them a great deal.

"Well," Bowden said, "I'd better brew up some nitro-glycerine if you want the eastern and western portals blown again."

"I do," Strobridge said. "With this kind of weather coming at us tonight, inside the tunnels is the best place for our workers. Just bring down a couple of tons of granite, Dr. Bowden. Enough to keep Crocker's Pets busy during the storm."

"When will you attempt to sled the locomotive and railroad construction cars over the summit?" Jessie asked.

"We'll start loading them on sleds tomorrow."

"Even if there is a blizzard?"

Crocker nodded. "We can't afford to wait a single day. The Donner Party, as you recall, stopped just blow the summit—as we are now. Had they pushed on late into

146

the night, they would have topped the summit and managed to get down to help in Sacramento. But they waited one extra night, and that was their disastrous mistake. We will not wait one hour to begin our effort to get that locomotive and those railroad cars onto the eastern slopes of these mountains."

"I see," Jessie said, knowing the railroad man was correct, because this storm might be followed by a series of storms, and in a week, the summit could be blanketed with forty or fifty feet of fresh snow, making the sledding effort much more dangerous and difficult.

Bowden shuffled off to do his work on the western portal before the weather deteriorated any further. Jessie wondered what would happen to the man if an accidental explosion killed a lot of innocent Chinamen. She suspected that Bowden might not be able to stand up under that kind of burden.

As if reading her thoughts, Strobridge said, "He'll be fine, Miss Starbuck."

"But what about after this summit tunnel is finished?"

"We'll use him all the way across Nevada," Crocker said. "We'll use his nitroglycerine to blast us a railroad clear into Utah Territory. And after that, there will be other railroads to build and tunnels to blast. A man like Dr. Bowden, he may never be allowed back into his San Francisco laboratory, but he'll also never have to worry about being unemployed."

Jessie sighed. "I just hope that he or someone else discovers a new formula that will be safer to use. Seems to me that even as careful as he is, sooner or later. . . ."

Jessie didn't need to finish her statement, because the result of an accident was obvious. Besides, the time for conversation was past. She and Ki would need to hurry

147

if they were to be ready to catch the supply train down to Sacramento.

It seemed to Jessie that the next few days would be critical to either the success or failure of the Central Pacific Railroad. One thing for sure, she was very glad to have the samurai at her side once again.

★

Chapter 18

Jessie and Ki rode the Central Pacific construction supply train down from Donner Pass, where a blizzard was howling. Even though it was almost midnight when they arrived, it was too warm in Sacramento for snow. Instead, a cold rain was falling as Jessie and Ki hurried toward the construction crews that worked frantically to load and chain down a completely dismantled locomotive onto no less than five flatcars.

"Who is in charge here?" Jessie asked one of dozens of workmen holding lanterns aloft in the rain.

"Over there," the man pointed. "The foreman's name is Hugh Banks. But who the hell are. . . . "

Jessie did not wait to explain. Trudging through the mud, heads low and trying to keep the rain out of their eyes, she and the samurai approached the man that had been pointed out to her.

"Are you in charge?"

"That's right," Banks said. "But I ain't got time to talk right now. You want to talk, come by my office tomorrow morning after this train is gone. Then, I'll talk."

"I'm here because Mr. Strobridge and Mr. Crocker thought I should be," Jessie said, glancing toward a tin

149

shed that would at least afford them some comfort from the downpour. "And I must speak to you for a few minutes. It's very important."

"So is getting this locomotive boiler on that flatcar without an accident," Banks growled.

Jessie could see that the man was not going to be cooperative. She turned to the samurai and said, "Will you please escort Mr. Banks over here under the shed and make him understand that I must speak with him for a few minutes?"

Ki nodded and stepped forward. His iron grip fastened on the railroad foreman's arm, and his thumb dug into a nerve that brought Banks up on his toes.

"Hey!" he cried weakly. "What the hell are you doing?"

The samurai applied even more pressure. "Miss Starbuck is a lady, and what she has to say is more important than anything you have to do in the next few minutes. Is that understood?"

Hugh Banks nodded his head up and down very rapidly. "Let go of my arm!"

"Then you'll come along quietly?"

"Yes!"

Ki released the foreman and followed him over to see Jessie. Banks was furious, but Ki had made him a believer, and he was not going to say anything rash with the samurai standing at his elbow.

"All right, you got two minutes, lady. What the hell is it that can't wait until morning?"

"We believe that someone will try to sabotage this train and destroy the locomotive you and your men have worked so hard to dismantle and load on those flatcars."

Banks frowned. "Now why should anyone do that?"

150

"Because they want the Central Pacific to go bankrupt," Jessie said. "And it will if Congress becomes convinced that the summit tunnel cannot be completed."

"Oh, but it will be! They've a scientist up there now using nitroglycerine."

"I know that," Jessie said. "I'm the one that went to San Francisco and brought him to the Sierra camp."

"Then what. . . . "

"Listen," Jessie said sternly. "Have you hired men to ride guard on these flatcars?"

"I had some, but I thought when the blizzard struck that the run up the mountain would be delayed until the weather cleared."

"Then you have no guards?"

Banks squirmed a little. "I only just now learned that our locomotive was going up in the morning. That's why we're still working at this hour! It's madness to go up in this weather! What the hell are Crocker and Strobridge thinking about?"

"They want to use the weather in hopes that it will make a sabotage attempt impractical."

"So that's it," Hugh grumbled. "Well, I tell you what—if the weather is as bad up on that mountain as it looks, this train won't even reach the pass. I've had a snowplow bolted on the lead engine, but even that might not be enough. It's a hell of a weight going up this mountain, I'll tell you."

"If we get snowbound," Jessie argued, "Crocker will send an army of Chinese down to dig us out. It won't be easy, but possible. What worries us is that someone will try to blow a trestle just as the train is crossing and send everything into a gorge."

"In this weather?"

"Why not? A fuse will burn if placed up under a tres-

151

tle, out of the wind and snow."

"Sure, but. . . . "

"Then we'll have to inspect every trestle before crossing," Jessie said.

Banks shook his head. "Lady, it would be impossible to make an inspection up there in a driving snowstorm. If you didn't slip and fall to your death off the trestle, you'd freeze. I wouldn't ask my worst enemy to inspect those trestles in this kind of weather."

"Thanks," Jessie said. "How soon will the train be leaving?"

"I'm shooting for daybreak. We'll be using three locomotives. But even that might not be enough to get through the snow, especially if we've had a few avalanches."

Avalanches. Jessie had not even considered them until now. "How many men will be on the train?"

"Three locomotive engineers and their firemen, along with four others riding along to keep an eye on things."

"Will they be armed?"

"No."

"Arm them," Jessie said.

Banks clenched his fists. "And if I don't?"

"If you don't and we are attacked by saboteurs, you will be at least partially responsible," Jessie said with growing impatience.

Banks looked as if he had swallowed a frog and was about to choke, but he managed to say, "All right. I'll have four armed men assigned to watch for mechanical trouble. But if I tell them they might be attacked, I expect they'll refuse to go."

"That's a chance we must take," Jessie said. "Ki and I will do the trestle inspections, but we're going to need armed men backing us who are not afraid to fight."

"Anything more?" Banks demanded.

"Just one thing," Jessie said. "Are you always as unpleasant to deal with, or is it just that your mood matches the nasty weather?"

Banks started to cuss her out, but when Ki stepped in closer, he thought better of the idea and stomped off into the mud and the falling rain.

"I think," Jessie said, "that we had better be prepared to fend for ourselves. If his men reflect his attitude, then we're going to be on our own all the way to Donner Pass."

Ki agreed. "I will ride with that huge boiler," he said. "That's the most important part of the locomotive and the one that saboteurs would be most interested in seeing destroyed."

"You're right about that," Jessie said. "They come from Boston, all the way around Cape Horn. But you'd freeze to death riding on a flatcar next to the thing."

"I'll climb inside of it for cover. When the train stops at each trestle, I'll jump out again."

Jessie reluctantly agreed to the plan. "All right, but one thing that Mr. Banks said did make sense, and that is that we'll both need some heavier clothing if we're to survive up there. Let's go find some."

"Yes. And we'll need a couple of rooms. I need to get a little sleep before daybreak. There's nothing we can do tonight except try and be as alert tomorrow as we can. I have a feeling that we will both be tested to our limits."

Judging from exterior appearance, the Delta Saloon and Hotel was not the kind of establishment in which Jessie would have chosen to spend the night. However, given the lateness of the hour and the fact that her teeth were chattering and she was soaked to the bone, she decided to look no farther.

153

When she and Ki walked into the downstairs saloon, their presence caused heads to turn, and Ki judged it a very rough crowd.

"I don't see a registration desk," Jessie said. "We'd better ask the bartender if they have any vacant rooms."

"Yeah," the bartender said a few minutes later, "you say you want separate rooms?"

"That's right," Ki said.

The bartender studied Jessie and he shook his head. "Whatever you want. But it'll cost you five dollars each. Those rooms keep pretty busy, if you know what I mean."

"As long as they are clean," Jessie said, "and unoccupied."

"Oh, hell yeah they are," the bartender said, pointing to the stairs. "Go on up and take the last two rooms on the right of the hall. Numbers four and five." He gave them a pair of room keys and said, "Checkout time is at noon."

"We'll be gone before the sun rises," Jessie said, heading for the stairs.

They met a young saloon girl and her man in the upstairs hallway. The girl would have been pretty if her eyes hadn't been red and puffy from crying. The man who held her arm was jerking her around and cuffing her hard.

"Next time you sass me I'll knock your damn head off!" he snarled. "And if you ever even look at another man again, I'll kill you!"

"Wes, you don't own me!" the girl sobbed. "I don't love you and I never have. Let me alone!"

Wes was a tall, heavyset man who had once probably been handsome but who had not aged well. In his mid-thirties, he had a roll of fat around his waist and a double chin. But he was big and strong and obviously mean.

154

"Why you little. . . . "

Ki stepped in front of Jessie. "I think the lady wants you to clear out," he said.

Wes twisted around to face the samurai. "You lookin' for a busted head too?"

"No," Ki said. "But the lady wants you to leave her be. I think you'd better do as she asks."

The girl sniffled. "Mister," she said, "I'm grateful for your wanting to help, but there's no sense both of us getting hurt. You'd better just leave us be."

"No," Ki said, "I can't do that."

Wes shoved the girl hard back through her open doorway, and Ki heard her crash into something and hit the floor. The samurai had heard enough, and when Wes came at him, Ki felt a surge of anticipation.

Wes looped a roundhouse right that had all the speed of a swinging barn door. Ki ducked and chopped the big man in the kidneys as he struggled to keep his balance. Wes grunted with pain and struck the wall, then turned and lunged at Ki.

The samurai easily sidestepped the much slower man and used a sweep kick to knock Wes sprawling across the floor. While the man was still struggling to rise, Ki drove a snap-kick into his face and broke his nose. When Wes buried his face in his hands, Ki knew the fight was over.

"Get out of here," he said. "And leave the girl alone."

Wes struggled to his feet and staggered toward the stairway, cursing and moaning.

Ki turned to Jessie. "I will wake you before dawn."

"Thank you," Jessie said, using her key to go into her room.

When Ki was sure that Jessie was safe behind a locked door, he turned around and stood by the girl's doorway. "Are you all right?"

She was on the floor and her face was bruised. "Not really," she said. "But I thank you for your help. Wes is going to be back up here pretty soon, and I'm afraid it will go even worse for me than before."

"Then why don't you leave?" Ki asked.

"It's storming out tonight, and I've no money or place to sleep. Besides, he'd just hunt me down in the morning."

"Then you'll let him beat you again?"

"Unless I've got a better choice," the girl said, climbing to her feet and straightening her hair. "Can I stay with you?"

Ki frowned. "I'm leaving before daybreak."

"Please let me go with you."

"You can't. I'm riding a flatcar up to Donner Pass."

"In this weather?" The girl frowned. "Just take me up the tracks to Cisco. I've got friends there and Wes will never find me."

"All right," Ki said. "But you'll have to ride up with me in a locomotive boiler."

"A what?"

"Never mind," Ki said quietly.

"Can we sleep in your room so Wes can't find us tonight?"

"Sure," Ki said. "Grab your things."

The girl's name was Polly, and it took her less than a minute to pack a bag and hurry across the hallway to Ki's room. They locked the door, and ten minutes later, Ki and the girl were climbing into a narrow bed.

"I want to thank you for helping me," she said, kissing his face.

"No thanks are necessary. You don't have to. . . ."

The girl kissed his protest away, and Ki took her in his arms. She was soft and warm and he was hard and

156

cold. She shivered as their bodies came together, and when Ki spread her legs apart, she found his manhood and guided him into her.

"Do you always act so gallantly?" she asked, unbuttoning her nightgown so that he could suck on her breasts.

"I don't like to see men hurt women," Ki said, his hips starting to move against hers. "Especially women like you."

Polly moaned when his tongue flicked at her nipples. "Wes never did that," she panted. "All he did was climb on me and take his own satisfaction. It was always over in a couple of minutes."

Ki prided himself on bringing pleasure to his partner in lovemaking. His fingers reached down to touch the place of their union, and he found the bud of her greatest pleasure. His long fingers stroked this bud while his manhood worked in and out, bringing Polly to a writhing frenzy.

"Oh, oh!" she cried. "I never had a man that took it so slow and nice!"

Ki smiled and did not stop pleasuring her until she began to thrash and her heels were raking the sheets. She cried out, and her hands gripped his plunging buttocks, drawing all of him inside of her.

"Yes! Oh, yes!" she gasped as her body stiffened with release.

A moment later, the samurai also found his release as he emptied his seed inside of her.

They lay panting in an embrace for a long time, until the samurai rolled off the girl and climbed to his feet. He walked over to a basin of water and poured himself a drink.

Polly smiled. "You are a beautiful man," she said. "Thanks."

"You're welcome," Ki replied, "and. . . . "

Whatever he was about to say ended when the door crashed open and there stood Wes with his broken nose stuffed with cotton, a gun in one fist and a bottle of whiskey in the other.

"Say your prayers," he hissed, cocking the hammer of his gun.

In one swift motion Ki hurled the glass of water that he'd been drinking. It caught Wes in the mouth and his gun exploded, driving a bullet into the floor.

Polly screamed, and before Wes could raise his gun and fire, Ki lifted a *shuriken* star blade from his clothes and threw it hard.

The blade buried itself in the big man's forehead. The six-gun dropped from Wes's hands. His eyes rolled up, and he staggered back into the hallway, trying to pull the blade out of his skull.

He was still trying when he slammed into the wall and then slid down to the floor and rolled over on his side. Ki plucked his *shuriken* blade from the man's head and wiped it on his shirt.

"You should have quit while you could," he said. "I gave you a second chance."

Polly jumped up and raced to the door. She pulled Ki back inside the room, then locked the door and threw herself into Ki's arms, weeping with relief.

"Don't worry," Ki said. "It's over with for you now."

After a few minutes, she got control of herself. She sniffled and gazed up into his eyes. "Make love to me again," she begged. "Give me your strength one more time before we leave for Cisco."

Ki's arms enfolded her. "It will be my pleasure," he whispered as he led the shaken saloon girl back to his bed.

Chapter 19

Ki, Jessie and Polly bought heavy winter coats and gloves right off the backs of some railroad workmen who were just finishing their work of loading and tying down the dismantled locomotive engine.

It was daybreak, but there was no sunrise, just a pitiful light seeping out of the east. The sun was hidden behind the heavy storm clouds, and if anything, the weather had actually deteriorated since their arrival the night before.

"All aboard!" the engineer shouted as he blasted his steam whistle and his fireman shoveled coal like a man possessed.

Jessie climbed up into the cab of the lead locomotive while Ki and Polly prepared to head for the boiler.

"Cisco is only a few miles up the line," Jessie said just before they separated. "If the weather is too bad, then come on up here. You'll be no help if you're half-frozen."

Ki nodded. He had been thinking the same. "Let's just hope all we have to fight today is the bad weather," he said, taking Polly's hand and leaving.

When the Central Pacific supply train pulled out of Sacramento it was raining hailstones the size of eggs and the American River was already cresting in the lowest places.

Jessie positioned herself between the engineer and the fireman, whose job it was to keep the steam pressure at its maximum safety level. On a climb such as they were about to undertake, over two hundred pounds of coal would be consumed in the firebox each mile, and it took a powerful man to move that much fuel.

"At least it stays warm in here," Jessie said, cradling her rifle and staring straight ahead at the heavy clouds that blanketed the mountaintops.

"Warm?" the engineer shouted, giving the train full power as they pulled a steady upgrade toward Cisco. "You damn right it'll stay warm! I'll bet we ain't going to make it to the top, though. Not in this weather."

"Maybe not," Jessie said as the fireman shoveled coal like a madman, "but Mr. Crocker and Mr. Strobridge are expecting us to try."

The engineer, a crusty old veteran in his early sixties, told her, "We got power enough to pull the weight, no doubt about that part of it, but we'll play hell beating our way through the snowdrifts near the summit if they're as deep as I expect 'em to be."

"How far to the first trestle?" Jessie asked.

"Ten miles."

"I want you to stop."

"What?"

Jessie had been afraid of this kind of reaction. "I guess that Mr. Banks didn't tell you that we're expecting we might be sabotaged on this trip."

Even the fireman stopped shoveling to stare at her.

"What the devil are you talking about?" the engineer demanded. "If we stop on this mountainside, we lose all our momentum. Be a hell of a lot harder to pull the grade."

"There's no choice," Jessie said, looking at both men. "We expect that one of the trestles might be rigged with explosives."

The fireman, a burly fellow stripped down to his waist and with forearms as thick as saplings, growled, "I make two-forty a day, ma'am. The engineer earns four dollars. But even he ain't being paid to take big risks."

"We'll do the best we can," Jessie said. "Crocker and Strobridge are counting on us to bring this locomotive to the work camp. They've been constructing sleds, and I'm sure they've been working all night in a blizzard to be ready for us. The least we can do is to try and be there on time."

The fireman and the engineer exchanged worried glances, and the engineer said, "All right, but if we could at least keep rolling a little bit, I think it would make a big difference."

"Fair enough," Jessie said. "You'll be stopping at Cisco, won't you?"

"Nope," the engineer said. "No reason to in this weather. Won't be any passengers getting on or off."

"That's where you are wrong," Jessie said. "We've got one."

When the train had labored into Cisco, Ki helped Polly out of the boiler and off the train. Their lips were half-frozen as they kissed and Ki said, "Find a new line of work. One safer. Here's some money to tide you over until you can get back on your feet."

He shoved two hundred dollars into her pocket, and she tried to hold him a moment longer, but he pried himself loose and ran forward in the swirling snow until he came to the lead locomotive. Swinging up inside the cab, he came face to face with Jessie.

161

"What's wrong?" she asked.

"Nothing," Ki replied. "But even dressed like an Aleut hunter, I'm still half-numb from the cold. I think I'll ride up front with you."

Jessie was pleased to have him close. "Did you give Polly the money?"

"Yes. And I think I've convinced her that she must find a new line of work. Hopefully, that money will be what she needs to get a fresh start."

Jessie hoped so too. Saloon girls and prostitutes had no future, only a premature death either by disease or at the hand of some drunken or jealous brute.

The train pulled out of Cisco and continued up the mountain. Snow had replaced hail, and it was falling heavily. Even though it was day, as they labored up through the narrow cuts and under the drooping trees covered with snow, the visibility was only a few hundred feet, and the giant snowplow mounted to their cowcatcher had already begun to whip a stream of snow off to each side of the roadbed.

The engineer was grim. "If we're scrapin' snow at this elevation, we'll be buried at a couple of thousand more feet."

Jessie and Ki said nothing. Once, Ki offered to spell the heavily perspiring fireman for a while, but the burly man shook his head and kept working like a machine.

"First trestle is just ahead," the engineer told them, "and I'm going to slow her down but keep moving ahead a little so we don't lose momentum. I'm signaling the engines behind me to do the same."

The engineer blasted his steam whistle several times, and the fireman stopped shoveling coal for a few minutes as the train inched ahead at a crawl.

"Let's go," Jessie said, gripping her rifle and step-

162

ping out into the storm, then leaping into a thick layer of snow.

Ki landed right beside her, and they both trotted ahead of the locomotive, slipping and sliding up to the trestle. There were no tracks in the snow to indicate that anyone had recently been here to set an explosive from the west end. But both Jessie and Ki knew that an absence of tracks was not guarantee enough. So they carefully moved out onto the trestle, taking great pains not to slip and fall. When they reached the center of the trestle, they both stretched out fully across the rail and then leaned out over the edge, staring through the falling snow to see if any unusual packages were attached to the wooden underpinnings.

"Nothing on this side," Ki shouted.

"Nor on this one," Jessie said as Ki helped her back on her feet. They moved carefully on across the trestle, and when the snowplow had passed, they jumped back up into the lead locomotive and huddled close to the firebox for warmth.

"There's another trestle about two miles up," the engineer growled. "Seems damned unlikely to me that anyone would be out trying to set explosives in this kind of weather."

"Are you ready to gamble your life and the lives of everyone else on that flimsy assumption?" Jessie asked.

The engineer's lips were crimped down at the corners, and he barked at the fireman to shovel faster.

The second trestle was higher, and when Jessie and Ki edged out on it, they could both feel the wind buffeting the underbraces.

"No tracks!" Ki shouted into the storm.

Jessie nodded. She carried a rifle in one hand and used it to balance herself as she moved out onto the icy trestle.

163

The footing was treacherous, and gusts of wind stuck her full force. Ki was yelling something and motioning for her to crawl as he was doing.

Moving across the trestle was an entirely forgettable experience, and when Jessie finally leaned over the side of the trestle, her teeth were chattering and she could hardly see, because the hard, cold wind was blowing snow directly into her eyes.

But right under her, she saw a dark package, and then she noticed the fuse.

"Ki!" she yelled. "Ki!"

He twisted around with a similar package in his fist, and when he started to shout a warning, Jessie saw a patch of snow erupt close by, as if a bullet had struck it.

She ripped the explosive out from under the trestle and searched in vain for a target.

A second bullet plucked at her sleeve, and the samurai was up and racing forward into the storm. Jessie could not see whoever was shooting at her, and the rifle shots were very faint.

"To hell with it!" she gritted as she unleashed a bullet off toward a snowy mountainside, hoping it might drive the ambushers from cover.

Almost a full minute passed before Jessie caught sight of Ki plunging forward through the snow. A heavy gust of blowing snow obscured him from her vision for several minutes, and then he reappeared higher up on the mountainside, and she thought she saw him waving for her to come join him.

Jessie didn't need much urging to get off the exposed trestle. Behind her and no doubt unaware that the trestle had been rigged with explosives and that a rifleman had opened fire, the engineer was creeping forward, blasting his steam whistle.

and hurried forward. When she finally reached solid earth again, it was a welcome feeling.

Ki bulled his way down the mountainside through the trees, and he was covered with snow.

"They were there," he said, his breath creating clouds of steam. "But they had snowshoes and went over the hill through some deep drifts that I sank to my neck in."

"We've got to get you up into that cab beside the firebox and get these wet clothes off before you catch pneumonia."

Ki did not argue. His teeth were already chattering. Jessie helped him up into the locomotive cab and shoved the package of explosives at the skeptical engineer.

"Maybe now you'll believe someone wants this train to end up down in a river gorge."

The engineer stared at the package. "It's black powder and a fuse. How were they ever going to . . . ?"

Jessie had already asked herself the same question, and there seemed to be only one logical answer. "There must have been several of them working together, and they'd planned to use hand signals. But in this storm, they couldn't get the messages up the line, and so the fuses were never lit."

The engineer nodded. "For God's sake, don't let this stuff near the firebox. There's enough powder there to blow us all to kingdom come."

Jessie pulled open the door of the cab and hurled the package out into the storm. She turned around and helped Ki strip down to his *cache-sexe*, a broad cotton band that he wrapped around his waist and then under his crotch. Ki's body was steaming, and so was his wet, icy clothing piled on the floor of the cab.

On impulse, Jessie gave the samurai a kiss on the

cheek. "There *has* to be easier ways of making a living than working for me," she said as the fireman kept shoveling coal and a fine black dust began to coat the wet and shivering samurai.

Ki nodded. "There were two riflemen," he said over the roar of the engine. "I didn't see them, but one was a very big and heavy man from the depression of his snowshoes. Maybe he's the same man that tried to kill you at the presidio."

"I wouldn't doubt it at all," Jessie said, grabbing up the samurai's clothing and looking for places to hang it in the warm cab, so that it would quickly dry. "Do you think they'll try that again?"

Ki shook his head.

Jessie tossed Ki's pants over a steam gauge and said to the engineer, "How many trestles do we have to cross before we reach the construction site below Donner Summit?"

"Six. All of 'em higher and more dangerous than that last one."

Jessie decided the wisest thing to do was for her to climb out to the snowplow and ride it across each trestle, peering ahead for any sign of foul play. But no more of this trying to hang over the side and peer underneath business.

It was just too cold and too dangerous.

Chapter 20

Somehow, the three locomotives had managed to power the heavily laden flatcars up to the Central Pacific Railroad construction site just below Donner Pass.

They were greeted by the no less than two thousand Chinese, who immediately began to help unload the dismantled locomotive and then reload it onto the huge wooden sleds that Crocker and Strobridge had ready and waiting.

While this was being done, Jessie and Ki were escorted into Crocker's executive car. They were shivering with the cold, and Crocker poured them each a stiff shot of brandy.

"I understand that you were attacked," the railroad construction boss said grimly.

"That's right," Jessie replied. "Ki and I found two explosives charges strapped under the second trestle. We don't know if the saboteurs had a foul-up in their communications or if they thought they were going to try and detonate the explosives with bullets as we crossed over the gorge."

"And you couldn't see our enemies?"

"No," Ki said. "I tried to go after them, but without snowshoes. . . ."

"I understand," Crocker said, lighting his cigar and staring out into the snowstorm. "I've decided to wait this blizzard out, and the moment it is over, we'll start pulling the sleds up and over Donner Pass. If we started tonight, I'd lose too many good men to pneumonia or frostbite."

"Of course," Jessie said. "How is the summit tunnel progressing?"

"Better than Harvey or I had dared to expect," Crocker said. "Your man, Bowden, he's working miracles up there on the summit. My engineers have calculated that he's only about sixty feet from punching all the way under the pass. The eastern and western portals should connect in another week or two at the most, then it will take a couple of additional months to widen the tunnel and lay tracks. We'll be rolling into Reno by spring, barring some catastrophe."

"You mean some disastrous act of sabotage," Jessie said.

"That's right," Crocker said in agreement. "I don't suppose you'd care to hazzard a guess as to where or when an attack might come."

Jessie looked to the samurai. "Ki?"

"I think," Ki said, "our enemies will strike on the summit. My guess is that they will try to simultaneously sabotage both the summit tunnel and our efforts to get that dismantled locomotive over Donner Pass."

"I agree," Crocker said. "Therefore, I think we can expect that the attack will come tomorrow—weather permitting. That being the case, we must be especially vigilant."

"We'll be out there waiting and watching," Ki promised.

"Good," Crocker said. "I'll also have a few sharpshooters with high-powered rifles standing guard."

Jessie felt the warmth of the brandy begin to take its effect. She did not decline Crocker's invitation for a refill, though Ki indicated that he had had enough.

"How far is it from here to the tracks already being laid in Truckee Canyon?" Jessie asked.

"About eight miles—four miles straight up the west slope and four more down the eastern slope," Crocker said. "It's going to be a major engineering feat. We've already tramped down a gulley through the deep snow, but with this latest storm, we'll have much more work to do as soon as the weather clears."

"And if it doesn't clear or it snows for weeks?"

Crocker jammed his cigar between his teeth and threw up his hands in exasperation. "I don't know," he admitted. "If this proves to be the same kind of blizzard that buried the Donner Party, then we might be out of luck and simply have to wait until the summit tunnel is finished. But that would be disastrous for us. We'd lose months of precious tracklaying to the Union Pacific. I don't even want to think about that as a possibility."

Jessie understood. "Then all we can do is to rest and wait to see what the weather will bring tomorrow. One thing is for certain, if we can't move, neither can our enemies."

Just three miles away, hidden near the summit, Roland Cross huddled beside Guito Perron and stared at their campfire. Through the mouth of their cave, Cross could see a few stars in the night sky, and he got excited.

"Look, Guito," he said, "the storm is passing!"

Guito Perron was a huge Spaniard, and when he climbed stiffly to his feet and moved to his partner's side, his swarthy face reflected absolutely nothing. "Then we will finish them this day," he said, turning back to the fire, where he had been oiling his hunting rifle.

"Yes," Cross said. "We will either finish them—or they will finish us. You know that we cannot go home again unless we are successful."

Guito looked up from his rifle. "We have no homes. Not since we met with Juarez and agreed to all this. If we fail, we will be hunted down and eliminated. You know that."

Cross nodded. "It is the samurai and the woman who are to blame," he said bitterly. "It was they who killed our best men in Wyoming, and now they have killed more in California. I should have spent more effort on them from the beginning. I should have made eliminating them our *first* order of business, instead of our second."

"There is no sense in thinking about what we should have done," Perron said. "We have both had our chances. I think the woman's beauty has blinded us, eh?"

Cross had to smile as he came back to huddle beside the campfire. "I have to admit this is true. Once, when I had her in my rifle sights, I could not bear to pull the trigger and send a bullet through one of her beautiful breasts. It would have been like defacing a work of art."

"Ha!" the hulking Spaniard said. "A work of art does not put our necks on the block to be chopped off like those of stewing chickens. We must kill them all. The woman, the samurai, Crocker and Strobridge. All of them!"

Cross nodded. "It will be done today," he vowed. "And we will take many more with them."

Perron looked up, a question on his face. "How?"

"I will show you later," Cross said. "But before daylight, we have work to do."

Perron was not pleased. "I do not like surprises," he

rumbled. "I think you had better tell me what you have in mind now. That way, if you are killed. . . well, if such a misfortune should occur, then I would still have the benefit of your idea."

Cross removed a silver cigarette case from his coat pocket. He took out an expensive brown cigarette, lit it and exhaled into their campfire.

"Very well," he said finally. "What I propose to do is to pay a visit to our chemist friend and have him make us a special surprise. One that will cause an avalanche to bury everything in its path. And by everything, I think you can guess what I mean."

Guito Perron smiled with appreciation. "This is a fine idea! It would be so simple that I wonder why I did not think of it myself. We simply let the mountain do our killing and even the burying."

"Yes," Cross said. "Now let us put on our snowshoes and go find the chemist before daylight."

"We will have to kill the guard to reach him," Guito said. "But this I can do very quietly."

The powerful Spaniard removed a garrote from his jacket. It was made of wire, very thin and light but also very strong. Cross watched the man snap it tight several times, and he involuntarily shivered. Guito, for all his size and outward calm, was a crazy man when it came to strangling his enemies.

Cross and Guito Perron managed to slog their way to the summit. At daybreak, they slipped up near the cabin where Dr. Bowden lived and made his nitroglycerine early each morning for use in the summit tunnel. The pair had worked together for many years, first in Europe as terrorists, then later they had taken on larger and bolder enterprises, until now they were masterminding the plot to destroy the transcontinental railroad. Investors had been found to purchase an alternate route, one much farther south that would benefit the Mexican revolutionary Juarez as well as a few unscrupulous Southerners.

"You take the guard over there," Cross said, pointing to the trees. "I'll see if any others are inside, and then I'll get the doctor before he can cause us any more mischief."

Guito nodded and went into a crouch. He slipped through the heavy snow toward a guard that was huddled under a crude wooden shelter. Guito came around behind him as silent as a panther. When he was very close, he stepped out of his snowshoes and then rushed the man.

The snow did hinder his charge, but even at that, the guard, who was half-frozen and half-asleep, never had a chance. Guito's garrote flipped over the guard's head, and the man died kicking and choking as the big Spaniard held him facedown in the snow. When the man was dead, Guito turned to see that Cross had already entered the cabin.

"Let go of me!" Bowden screamed.

Cross struck the scientist across the face. "Shut up and finish making that batch of nitroglycerine."

"Never!"

Cross grinned as Guito filled the doorway. "I guess we'll have to teach you some obedience, Dr. Bowden. Close the door, Guito. We have a few minutes to spare, and I don't think it will take much longer than that to show the good doctor how you kill with your little piece of wire."

Guito smiled and dangled the silver wire before Bowden's eyes. It was covered with blood, and it made Bowden gasp with fear and buckle at the knees.

"Guito, why don't you see how it fits around the doctor's neck?"

Guito stepped forward, and Bowden shrank away in abject terror. "What . . . what are you going to do with the nitroglycerine?"

Cross shook his head. "We don't intend to do anything but blow up the summit tunnel."

Bowden stared at the bloody wire and the powerful hands of the Spaniard. He was terrified, willing to believe almost anything.

"Listen," he heard himself whisper. "I . . . I want to cooperate, but. . . . "

"Guito?"

The Spaniard grabbed Bowden and snapped the wire around his skinny neck. He pulled it tight and Bowden's eyes bugged with fear.

"No!" he cried. "Not like this! I beg of you!"

"Then do as we ask," Cross said. "Now."

"Yes!" the scientist choked as the wire sawed at his throat. "Yes!"

Cross nodded, and Guito removed the wire to watch as the scientist groveled in terror at his feet. "We will need at least a pint of nitroglycerine."

Bowden looked up. "And you swear you won't kill any innocent men? Not even the Chinese workmen?"

"Of course not," Cross said in his most soothing voice. "There is no need. But we'll have to hurry before they get up here and see something is wrong, won't we?"

Bowden nodded eagerly. He struggled to his feet and rushed to his supplies. He would do exactly as they asked.

Chapter 21

The three men wearing snowshoes trudged silently through the forest, keeping off the summit so that they could not be seen by anyone down below.

The air was very thin and cold. The new-fallen snow was wet, and it clung to the snowshoes, making it difficult to cover ground with any speed. But finally they reached a point about a quarter of a mile upslope from the army of laboring Chinese.

"This will be perfect," Cross said, pulling the scientist down beside Guito Perron and himself.

"Guito, you and Bowden take enough nitroglycerine to blow up the summit tunnel. I'll use the rest to create an avalanche that will bury those sleds and that dismantled locomotive so deep their scrap metal won't be found until next spring."

Bowden was gagged, and he struggled to protest, but Guito backhanded him across the side of the head so hard that the scientist was laid out flat and completely stunned.

"Don't kill him yet!" Cross said angrily. "You'll need him to demonstrate how to set the tunnel charges. Otherwise, you've got no way to escape alive."

Guito reluctantly nodded as they both studied the scene far below.

Crocker and Strobridge were extolling their workers to pull and push the gigantic sleds and their massive cargo up toward the summit. Ropes three hundred feet long were covered by the hands of Chinese workmen who strained upward, foot by slippery foot. Hundreds more Chinese were pushing and pulling at the sleds from the sides and the rear. The lead sled held the precious locomotive boiler, and though it was not the heaviest load, it was the biggest.

"It's quite a magnificent sight, isn't it?" Cross said. "I almost hate to ruin their party."

"It's them or us," Guito said as he transferred several flasks of nitroglycerine into his own pouch to be carried into the summit tunnel.

Cross nodded. "Yeah, that's the only way we can afford to look at it. It isn't anything personal. It's just that I sure hate to bury that Starbuck woman. It's a terrible waste."

"Forget her!" Guito said impatiently. "Have you noticed that there are armed guards walking beside each sled? They're expecting an attack from us."

"I know," Cross said. "And I've also noticed that the samurai is nowhere in sight. We can just bet that he's not taking a siesta. He's looking for us, Guito. And I worry about him more than the whole lot of Crocker's hired riflemen."

"Let's get this over with," Guito said, picking up the unconscious scientist and throwing him over his shoulder.

"Wait a minute," Cross said, pulling out his pocket watch. "Let's both time our explosions for one hour from now. That way, whatever survivors there might be will

175

be running in every direction."

"And where will we meet?" Guito asked, comparing his own pocket watch to make sure they were synchronized.

"In Hangtown. One week from today."

Guito smiled and extended his hand. "Hangtown? Or perhaps in hell one hour from now, eh?"

"Perhaps," Cross said. "But if so, I mean to take a lot of Chinamen and one beautiful and very rich woman with me."

When Guito had left, Cross eased his corked flask of nitroglycerine down into the soft snow, and then he rolled in the wet stuff until he was covered from head to toe. Satisfied, he picked up the flask and began to slither downslope, his body very much below the level of the newly fallen snow. He was certain that he could not be spotted by anyone.

It took him longer than he had expected to reach the place where he would plant the nitroglycerine. His progress was hampered somewhat by his anxiety that he might actually initiate an avalanche that would result in his own death.

Cross was sweating with fear as he raised his head a little to judge the speed and angle of the ascending work party and their huge snow sleds. Satisfied that he was in position, he carefully packed snow around the flask and raised it up to surface level, where he could put it between his rifle sights. Now, it was time to retreat back up the gulley of snow he had created.

By the time he reached his vantage point and brushed the snow from his clothing, Cross was wet and shivering. He consulted his pocket watch. In just fifteen minutes, his bullet would detonate the flask of nitroglycerine and send a mountainside of snow cascading down to bury the Central Pacific Railroad once and for all.

Cross rubbed his hands together, trying to regain some feeling. He had never felt so cold, and his heart was pounding in his chest when he slithered over to his snowshoes. For almost five minutes he struggled to lace them back on his feet before he gripped his hunting rifle, inspected it carefully and then drew a practice bead on the nitroglycerine some fifty yards below.

Satisfied, he finally smiled, and longed for the steadying effect of a cigarette. Everything was going to work out just fine. Cross was very confident that the exploding nitroglycerine would cause tons of snow to break from the mountainside and hurtle down upon the workmen.

The only real concern he had was that Guito would be unable to successfully destroy the summit tunnel. But even if the big Spaniard failed completely, Cross knew that the avalanche he was about to create would be devastating to the Central Pacific Railroad. He would bury Crocker, Jessica Starbuck and about a thousand Chinese, and that many deaths would be enough to persuade Congress to withhold further funding on the Central Pacific Railroad.

An investigation would be held, and Crocker's bold plan to begin laying track on the eastern slope of the Sierras before he conquered Donner Pass would be revealed to the public. There were plenty of congressmen who would be outraged enough to kill this project.

Cross studied his watch. Just ten minutes to go.

Jessie could feel an evil presence. As she trudged along beside the Chinese and the huge, heavily laden sleds they pulled, she could sense that some terrible calamity was about to befall them.

Her green eyes kept raking the surrounding mountain-

177

side, looking for the enemy. An enemy she was certain would strike from the vantage point of higher ground.

And where was the samurai? She had not seen him for hours, though this did not surprise her. Was he up above or. . . .

Something caught Jessie's eye. The faintest of movements in the snow high up and just ahead. She stopped dead in her tracks.

"Mr. Crocker!" she shouted. "Stop everything!"

Crocker was in the lead, Strobridge was behind the sleds, urging his Chinese to pull with every ounce of their combined strength.

"Hold it!" Crocker shouted, raising his hands and looking to Jessie. "What is it?"

Jessie raised her finger, and thousands of pairs of eyes lifted to follow her gaze to the snowy slopes up above.

"There!" Jessie called. "Do you see him?"

They did.

"Fire!" Crocker bellowed. "Fire!"

Jessie's rifle was already slamming to her shoulder. She saw the man up above raise his own rifle. Dimly, she was aware that he had a telescopic sight, and only then did she fathom his terrible plan.

Jessie fired the first rifle bullet, but she missed because the saboteur was at the limits of her rifle range and the blinding snow and the mountainside made accurate shooting very difficult. But her bullet must have come very close, because the saboteur jumped sideways, and when he came up again to fire, he was cut down in a hail of bullets from all of Crocker's hired marksmen.

Jessie's second bullet was among those that felled the assassin, and when he pitched forward into the snow and began to tumble down the mountainside, he caused an avalanche to rush ahead of him.

178

The man's body disappeared, and everyone threw themselves behind the sleds and prayed that the entire snowpack above them would not break free. They listened to a loud hiss as tons of snow swept down and then passed just ahead, completely wiping out Crocker's tramped-out highway.

Jessie was one of the first to raise her head, and through the swirling snow she saw trees being snapped from their roots and swept down the slope. The avalanche had missed striking the lead sled and the precious boiler by no more than fifty feet.

"Son of a bitch," Crocker whispered. "That was close!"

Jessie nodded. "Unless I'm sadly mistaken, you'll find a flask of nitroglycerine up on the slope somewhere, which our man intended on detonating with a rifle bullet."

Crocker squinted up the slope. "Maybe there's more up there."

"If there were, they'd be doing what the first one failed to do," Jessie concluded. "I think that it's safe to go on, but I'm going to the summit tunnel. That's where Ki must be and. . . ."

"Listen!" Crocker shouted.

They all heard the distant sound of gunfire.

"Harvey!" Crocker shouted. "Carry on here!"

Strobridge nodded as his boss and Jessie took off running toward the tunnel.

Ki was waiting hidden beside the western portal of the summit tunnel when he saw the big Spaniard come hurrying forward at a crouch. Bowden was awake but still dazed, and the assassin carried him as easily as a sack of grain.

179

"That's far enough," Ki said, stepping out of his hiding place and standing before the tunnel's entrance. "You're not going any farther."

Guito Perron raised the flask of nitroglycerine. "I think you had better understand that I will not be stopped, Ki."

"You know me?"

Guito nodded. "I even expected you to find me. But still, I had hoped it would be after this work."

Ki studied the nitroglycerine. "I can't let you past and you can't turn around. So what is it you intend to do?"

"Kill you in a fight to the death," Guito said almost matter-of-factly as he carefully placed his nitroglycerine aside.

"Come on then," Ki said.

Guito dumped Bowden in the snow and pulled out his wire garrote and two heavy metal handles, each with spiked ends. He attached them with snap-hooks, and gripping one handle, he began to whirl the other round and round.

Ki decided that the match was entirely uneven, so he produced one of his own favorite fighting weapons, the *han-kei*, two heavy wooden sticks seven inches in length and attached by a horsehair braid. Gripping one handle, he also began to whirl the other.

The big Spaniard grinned with surprise. "This should be interesting."

Ki would not have used that term, but he supposed it fit. They began to circle. The Spaniard moved extremely well and Ki could see that the man was light on his feet.

"You could just surrender," Ki said. "You heard all that rifle fire and no explosion, so you know that your friend is dead by now and there is no way you can win."

"If I destroy this tunnel, I will win," Guito said. "But

if I do not, I will be killed anyway."

"By whom?"

"By men who hire men like me. Isn't it always that way?"

"But if this fails. . . ."

"Then they would turn their efforts to other parts of the world. Other grand schemes. Cross and I, we were the last they sent—and the best."

"Give it up. You could. . . ."

Ki did not have a chance to finish his offer, because Guito's massive arm snapped forward, and the heavy metal handle's spike caught the samurai on the forearm and opened it to the bone. But at the same instant, Ki's whirling *han-kei* struck the big man across the bridge of his hooked nose and broke it like an egg. Blood poured down Guito's face, but he made no sound.

"Give up," Ki said.

Instead, Guito hurled the wire and both handles at Ki's throat, but the samurai ducked and the garrote passed overhead. Ki slashed with the *han-kei*, and it connected solidly against the side of Guito's head. The big man staggered. Ki jumped forward and swept Guito's legs out from under him, but Guito still managed to hook his fingers into Ki's coat and pull him down.

They rolled over and over in the snow, and Guito, being so much heavier, had the best of it. The big man was ox-strong, and he kept slamming his bloodied face into Ki's face, trying his best to blind his opponent. Ki managed to get his hand between them, and his fingers dug for an *atemi* point, where he could put Guito to sleep.

"No!" Guito snarled as he reached for a gun hidden in his coat.

Ki knew that he had no chance of winning unless he killed the man and did it quickly. So with the heel of his right hand, he drove Guito's broken nasal bones up into his brain, and the Spaniard died instantly.

"Ki!"

The samurai rolled the dead Spaniard off of him and staggered to his feet as Jessie threw herself into his arms. Ki grinned at the overweight Crocker, who came lurching up, red-faced and out of breath.

"Careful," the samurai warned the railroad builder. "You're about to step on a pint of nitroglycerine and end all our cares in this world."

Crocker hopped up into the air and landed on both feet, just inches from the flask of nitroglycerine. "What the hell!"

Jessie stepped back. "Is it over?"

"Yes," Ki said. "He told me it was before he died. He was a brave man and a good fighter. I wanted to save him, but I couldn't. He was too strong."

Jessie looked at the samurai's forearm and frowned. She scooped up a handful of snow and placed it on the wound and said, "It's warm down in Texas, I'll bet."

"Warm would feel good."

Jessie laughed. Crocker laughed. The transcontinental race was on!

Watch for

**LONE STAR AND THE
GEMSTONE ROBBERS**

102nd in the exciting LONE STAR series
from Jove

Coming in February!

WESTERNS!

at least a savings of $3.00 each month below the publishers price. Second, there is never any shipping, handling or other hidden charges—Free home delivery. What's more there is no minimum number of books you must buy, you may return any selection for full credit and you can cancel your subscription at any time. A TRUE VALUE!

Mail the coupon below

To start your subscription and receive 2 FREE WESTERNS, fill out the coupon below and mail it today. We'll send your first shipment which includes 2 FREE BOOKS as soon as we receive it.